COUNTRY
LEGACY

AIDAN:
LOYAL COWBOY

NEW YORK TIMES BESTSELLING AUTHOR

Cathy McDavid

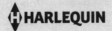
HARLEQUIN

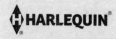

PLEASE RECYCLE
THIS PRODUCT IS RECYCLABLE

Recycling programs
for this product may
not exist in your area.

ISBN-13: 978-1-335-52345-7

Aidan: Loyal Cowboy
First published in 2012. This edition published in 2022.
Copyright © 2012 by Cathy McDavid

For questions and comments about the quality of this book,
please contact us at CustomerService@Harlequin.com.

Harlequin Enterprises ULC
22 Adelaide St. West, 41st Floor
Toronto, Ontario M5H 4E3, Canada
www.Harlequin.com

Printed in U.S.A.

Since 2006, *New York Times* bestselling author **Cathy McDavid** has been happily penning contemporary Westerns for Harlequin. Every day, she gets to write about handsome cowboys riding the range or busting a bronc. It's a tough job, but she's willing to make the sacrifice. Cathy shares her Arizona home with her own real-life sweetheart and a trio of odd pets. Her grown twins have left to embark on lives of their own, and she couldn't be prouder of their accomplishments.

To all the people who made this book possible. First, the five lovely and talented ladies who are my co-authors in this continuity—C.J. Carmichael, Roz Denny Fox, Shelley Galloway, Marin Thomas and Linda Warren. Your creativity amazes me, and I am truly honored to share this continuity with you.

It's true that behind every good author is a good editor. I've been fortunate to work with Kathleen Scheibling since I started writing for Harlequin. I can't thank you enough, Kathleen, for all the opportunities you've given me and all the faith you've placed in me. Writing books for Harlequin isn't just my job; it's my passion and a dream come true. I'm also delighted to have worked with Johanna Raisanen on this and the previous continuities. There isn't a more conscientious, more charming, more intelligent editor. Just how lucky can an author get?

Last, I must give a nod of appreciation to Walter Farley, author of the Black Stallion and Island Stallion series. The books I discovered in third grade led to a lifelong love affair with horses and, ultimately, *Aidan: Loyal Cowboy*.

Chapter 1

Mid-March in southeastern Montana was no time of year for a bucking horse auction. And yet, better than a hundred people had driven as many miles or more, braved ice-covered highways and trudged across acres of gray-brown slush, all in search of a bargain.

Ace Hart among them.

He stood with seven other potential customers, appraising the coal-black stallion and contemplating his finer qualities, which, at first glance, appeared in short supply.

The horse, slightly underweight for his intended use and a bit on the rangy side, had backed himself into the farthest corner of the pen. Ears flat, head stretched forward and nostrils flaring, he stomped a front hoof in the wet, mucky ground, flinging clumps of mud into the air. The customers took the horse's warning seriously and maintained a respectful distance, some of them scratching notes on the back of their bidding numbers for reference when the auction started.

Normally Ace would pass up a potentially aggressive horse like this one, outstanding bloodlines or not. But the animal's eyes, alert, inquisitive and highly intelligent, told Ace what he needed to know better than the AQHA registration papers taped to the pen railing.

This was no ordinary horse and no ordinary stallion.

The Midnight Express, or just plain Midnight as he was once known on the rodeo circuit, had been born to buck, his purpose in life to unseat any cowboy with nerve enough to ride him into the arena. Most of those rides had ended with the cowboy eating a face full of dirt.

No more.

If Ace purchased Midnight—make that *when,* he'd already decided the horse was his—he'd use Midnight exclusively for breeding purposes. Ace wasn't the kind of business manager or big-animal veterinarian to risk injuring a valuable investment.

"What do you think?" His mother came up beside him, linked an arm through his, then stuck her other hand in the pocket of her sheepskin-lined jacket.

"A little underweight. A little temperamental."

"But a beauty."

Indeed. Despite his ragged appearance, Midnight had all the potential Ace and his mother were seeking in a foundation stallion for their bucking horse breeding operation. He mentally calculated the top price they could afford to pay. With luck, the horse's prickly personality and poor condition would scare off other buyers.

"Howdy, Sarah. Ace." Earl McKinley, the Harts' neighbor and competitor in the bucking stock business, approached and fell in beside Ace's mother.

"Hello, Earl." She returned the greeting. "I didn't think you were coming today."

Neither had Ace. He glanced around, his throat suddenly dry.

Had Flynn accompanied her father to the auction? Told him about her and Ace?

Not likely. If Earl had any idea Ace spent the night with his daughter three weeks ago, he'd have a lot more to say to Ace than "howdy."

Just when Ace decided Flynn had stayed home, she appeared, casually approaching as if this was just another chance encounter with her neighbors.

"Flynn, good to see you," Ace's mother exclaimed.

"Hi, Sarah, how are you?" Flynn acknowledged Ace with a tilt of her head, the epitome of cool, calm and collected.

Not so Ace.

Sweat promptly broke out on his brow—both at the memory of the incredible night they'd spent together and his disgraceful exit the next morning.

What must she think of him?

Her demeanor gave nothing away.

She appeared to be concentrating on the conversation between his mother and her father.

At one time, the Harts and McKinleys had been fierce rivals. That changed to friendly rivals ten years ago when Ace's father died.

"Rumor has it you might be getting out of the business," his mother said to Earl.

"I haven't decided either way. If I can pick up a few head today at a good price, I may end up adding to my string. If not, I'll probably sell off. It's been a tough go the last few years, what with this economy."

"It certainly has."

"I heard you leased out three thousand acres to a cattle company from Missoula."

"We did. And sold off most of our cattle. We're down to three hundred head."

Earl whistled.

The recent recession and drop in the commodities market was a frequent topic among ranchers. Ace's mother was counting on the family's expanded bucking contracting business and reduced cattle operation to stabilize the ranch's shaky finances.

"I also hear you're planning to add to your string in a big way," Earl said.

"We are indeed." Her face lit up. "That's what brought us here."

"You thinking of buying this here fellow?"

All eyes went to the big horse in the pen.

"Considering it," Ace's mother answered coyly.

Earl's bucking string had always been significantly larger than the Harts' and included a dozen championship bulls and horses. If

Earl retired, that would certainly benefit the Harts and their plans.

From the glimmer of interest in Earl's eyes, he also saw and appreciated Midnight's potential.

Ace momentarily tensed. The old rivalry might just heat up again.

"I didn't know you were wanting a stud horse," he said.

"I like to keep all my options open." Earl's smile remained fixed, much like his daughter's.

She stood across from Ace, looking everywhere else but at him.

Well, he deserved her disdain. He'd messed up pretty bad.

That didn't stop him from missing her and wishing things were different.

"Shame about old Wally," his mother mused. Like most of the rodeo folk at the auction, she'd been acquainted with the late owner of the stock up for sale today. "He was a good man and will be missed."

"His kin must be in a hurry for their share of his money." Earl lifted his foot and examined the muddy water pouring off his galoshes, then stepped sideways to a spot that was only marginally less wet. "Couldn't they have postponed the sale six weeks till the weather improves?"

"They may have debts to pay off. Wally was sick a long time before he passed."

"More likely they didn't want to compete with the Miles City Bucking Horse Sale in May. Those kids of his never gave a flying fig about taking over his string even before he died. A shame, too." Earl shook his head. "He had some quality stock. Whoever those kids hired to care for these horses should be arrested."

"True." Ace's mother's gaze went from Midnight to the other horses on the next aisle over. "Some of them are faring rather badly, I'm afraid."

Earl made a sound of disgust. "I betcha this here horse couldn't buck off a ten-year-old boy."

Ace wouldn't take that bet. Midnight and the rest of Wally's string may have received less than adequate care in the two years since the old man fell ill, but Midnight possessed the heart of a champion and the spirit of a warrior.

He also had impeccable genes.

Earl knew it, too. He intentionally down-played his interest in purchasing Midnight by finding fault with him and the other horses. Ace's mother employed the same tactics with Earl. They'd been doing it for years, with Earl usually coming out ahead.

"You ready, sweetie?" Earl asked Flynn.

"Let's go."

"I'll be seeing you later when the auction starts." Earl tipped his hat at Ace's mother, then he and Flynn leapfrogged over wet patches to the double row of pens holding the geldings and mares.

The challenge had been officially issued.

"He's going to bid against us for Midnight," Ace's mother observed.

"He won't be the only one."

Ace watched Flynn go, ashamed at his relief. He should apologize to her. He owed her that much, if not more. But after three weeks without any contact, she'd probably refuse to speak to him, and he wouldn't blame her.

God, he'd been such an idiot.

"Aidan?"

"Yeah." His mother was one of the few people to call him by his given name.

"Are you going to examine that horse or what?" She inclined her head at the pen.

"I will. Eventually." He returned his attention to Midnight, forcing thoughts of Flynn from his mind. It wasn't easy.

It seemed as though the horse ignored everyone else except him. Good. They were of similar minds.

"Too muddy?" his mother asked. "Or is the horse too mean?"

"Unpredictable and wary aren't the same as mean." On the ranch and in his veterinarian practice, Ace had examined his share of mean horses. "He's a stallion standing within fifty feet of twenty mares. *His* mares. Not to mention the geldings. His competition, in his mind. He's in a strange environment, surrounded by strange people and hearing strange noises. He's bound to act a little temperamental."

"No one's been in the pen with him that I've seen."

"Are you challenging me?"

Ace's mother arched a brow at him and smiled. "When have you needed someone to challenge you other than yourself?"

He hadn't, not since his father died.

Eventually, Ace decided both he and Midnight were ready. He slipped the latch and opened the gate. The horse snorted and pawed the muck again, his way of saying, "You sure about this? Because I have a thousand pounds of solid muscle on you."

Ace was sure. He stepped inside the pen, shut the gate behind him and waited. When it came to horses, he had an endless supply of patience.

Now, people? Not so much.

"Easy, boy."

Midnight flicked his ears slightly at the silky smooth tone of Ace's voice but didn't budge.

"That's right."

Minutes ticked by, Ace wasn't sure how many. From the corner of his eye he noticed a small crowd had gathered in front of the pen. A few of the louder comments reached his ears.

"Watch this. You ever seen Hart at work?"

"He's got more nerve than me, climbing in with that brute."

"What is he? Some kind of horse whisperer or something?"

Not exactly, Ace thought. But he did have a knack for reading animals, horses especially, and for getting them to trust him. Enough to earn himself a reputation around the state.

When he sensed the moment was right, he

took a small, slow step forward. Midnight jerked his head, his gaze still fastened on Ace.

"There you go."

Another small step, this one met with an angry snort and a head toss. No problem. As long as the horse didn't show signs of charging him, Ace was okay.

"We'll do this on your terms, buddy."

Finally, Ace was close enough to touch the horse, though he hesitated.

"Good job," he murmured softly.

Midnight's breathing increased as he inhaled Ace's scent, the fine whiskers of his velvety nose brushing Ace's jacket sleeve. He was determined that the horse make the next move.

His patience, as usual, paid off.

Midnight sniffed Ace's hand, drew back and sniffed again.

It was a small but vital victory for Ace. When he reached out to stroke Midnight's neck, the horse flinched. He didn't bolt or rear, however, and after several more long moments, allowed Ace to run a hand along his neck and chest, his hide twitching.

Sadness squeezed Ace's heart. Neglect had scarred this magnificent animal. He just didn't understand some people, which would explain why, other than his family, he'd spent much of his thirty-four years a loner.

His attention wandered, as did his gaze. Flynn had evidently concluded one chance meeting with him was enough, for she was nowhere in sight. When Ace looked back around, Midnight had retreated to his corner and had resumed glaring at people. Ace in particular.

Rather than antagonize the horse unnecessarily, Ace conducted the remainder of his examination visually. Skittish personality and weight loss aside, the horse appeared in reasonably good health. Ace had no reason to doubt the copy of the medical report, which hung on the pen railing along with Midnight's registration papers.

Ace turned, his movements calm and measured. He was taking a big risk presenting his back to Midnight. He'd once met an old cowboy with a sizable chunk missing from his shoulder after just this sort of move. But Ace had to know for certain if Midnight was wary and not mean.

He walked unscathed to the gate and sighed quietly. On the other side, he paused to look at Midnight.

The horse bobbed his head.

Yeah, I agree. Ace grinned to himself, feeling as if he, too, had passed a test. *You're coming home to Thunder Ranch with me.*

His mother wasn't standing where he'd left her. Ace spotted her several feet away, conversing with his uncle Joshua and cousin Duke who'd accompanied Ace and his mother to the sale.

He'd barely started toward them when Flynn unexpectedly crossed his path. A jolt of alarm brought him to a halt.

"Hi," he muttered, trying to move. The soft ground pulled at him, sucking his boots down into the muck. He was trapped.

Served him right.

She stared at him in silence, tendrils of corn-silk-yellow hair peeking out from under her cowboy hat.

Memories surfaced. Ace had sifted his hands through that hair, watched, mesmerized, as the soft strands coiled around his fingers like spun gold.

Then, not two hours later, he'd abruptly left her bedside, hurting her with his transparent excuses.

No longer calm and collected, she stared at him with the same pained expression she'd worn that morning.

"Flynn, I'm sorry," he offered lamely.

"For what exactly?" She crossed her arms in front of her and glared at him through slitted blue eyes. "Slinking out of my room before my father discovered you spent the night, or acting like it never happened?"

Flynn thought she'd readied herself for their inevitable confrontation. All the phrases she'd used to bolster her defenses during the drive to the auction suddenly abandoned her, and she was once again an emotional weakling.

What had possessed her to sleep with him?

Easy. Ace had been her first love—unfortunately, a very one-sided first love. She'd invited him home, hoping to ignite that elusive spark with him at long last.

And she did.

For several hours his passion had burned brightly. Beautifully. Flynn had never been loved so intensely, so thoroughly. She'd told herself he must have genuine feelings for her, even if he didn't acknowledge them.

Reality, unfortunately, had returned when the sun crested the horizon, its soft rays breaching the blinds of Flynn's bedroom and vanquishing the cozy cocoon of night. Ace couldn't get dressed fast enough or leave in a bigger hurry. He'd had horses to check at home. A morning surgery scheduled. Then there was the meeting at the bank.

Legitimate excuses, but why hadn't he been able to look her in the face when he gave them? Or do more than kiss her forehead before escaping through the back door, sock-footed and boots in hand?

Because he hadn't wanted to stay with her or make a commitment.

Flynn had heard it all before. From her ex-husband and now Ace. The two men were peas in a pod. Both married to their jobs, both using their jobs as an excuse not to spend time with her.

Damn her foolish heart for always picking the wrong kind of man.

She should walk away from Ace, leave him the way he'd left her.

Instead, she stayed, his expression rooting her in place. If she wasn't still angry at him, she might have been swayed by the regret brimming in his incredibly dark brown eyes.

"Can we talk?" he asked. "I'd like to explain."

"This I have to hear."

"Not now, not here." He glanced over his

shoulder at the people milling nearby. "Later. Somewhere less crowded."

That was exactly what had gotten her into bed with him, his suggestion they leave the Number 1 Diner and go somewhere more private to continue their conversation.

Flynn rediscovered the confidence she'd lost upon first spotting Ace. "No, I don't think so."

"You have every right to be angry with me," he began slowly.

She cut him off. "Do you not own a calendar? You've had better than three weeks to explain. I'm either working at the emergency clinic or helping Dad with the horses. Finding me isn't a problem. Heck, I live next door to you."

"I'm a jerk."

His admission didn't soften her resolve. He'd wounded her when he hurried off that morning. Hurt her worse when he didn't call or come see her.

And she'd have walked barefoot across broken glass before calling him. Been there, done that—back when they'd dated briefly in college.

"Aidan!" his mother hollered. "We're heading over to inspect the mares and geldings."

She waved and smiled at Flynn. "Don't be a stranger. Come to lunch the next time Dinah's over."

Flynn waved in return. "Thanks." Her father and Ace's father might not have liked each other, but Sarah Hart had always treated Flynn like a second daughter.

And Ace had treated her like another little sister.

A four-year age difference hadn't helped. Not until she was in community college and he in vet school did he finally notice her as someone other than his sister Dinah's school chum.

They'd been careful in those days, keeping their relationship a secret in order to avoid their respective fathers' wrath. It was anyone's guess where things might have led if John Hart hadn't died and Ace's world hadn't crumbled.

"I need to go," he said.

"No one's stopping you."

It would be easier to hate him if he didn't appear contrite and miserable.

She'd seen him steady a full-grown steer as it collapsed to the ground. Cushion the animal with his body in order to spare it injury.

How could a man so big and strong and

capable be completely inept when it came to understanding women? No wonder he was still a bachelor.

Who was she to talk? She had one failed marriage behind her. A marriage that was, in all probability, a rebound from Ace.

"Flynn..." He reached for her.

"Forget it." She started toward the horse pens where her father waited, then hesitated. Squaring her shoulders, she turned and faced Ace. "You made a big mistake three weeks ago. You walked out on the best thing to happen to you in a long time."

She expected him to blush and falter and possibly be at a loss for words. That happened to him on occasion.

Today, he surprised her.

He met her stare head-on and said without missing a beat, "You're right."

Then why? her mind cried out.

When he said nothing else, she left, sniffing in an attempt to hold back her tears. She'd given him an opening, a chance to say he wanted to see her again, and he'd refused it.

When would she learn?

She'd come home to Roundup following her divorce, in large part because of Ace and the possibility that they could pick up where they'd left off.

Except they hadn't—a one-night stand years later didn't count—and, after today, it didn't appear as though they ever would.

Chapter 2

"Last up, folks, is the horse you've all been waiting for, The Midnight Express." Loud speakers mounted from poles on either side of the ring gave the auctioneer's voice a tinny and abrasive quality. "This here stud's lineage goes all the way back to the great hall-of-fame bucking horse Five Minutes to Midnight. He's won Bucking Horse of the Year twice, competed at the National Finals Rodeo a total of five times and has sired over sixty offspring, seven of which are actively competing on the rodeo circuit and doing well for their owners."

Flynn sat with her father in the aluminum

bleachers, listening to the auctioneer recite Midnight's selling points. The horse himself, however, had yet to make an appearance in the ring.

She fingered the flyer in her hand as they waited. Murmurings as to the reason for the holdup traveled through the crowd like a signal zipping along a cable. Her father's boot beat an agitated tattoo on the bleacher floor. He'd shown some interest in a few of the other bucking horses up for sale but let them all go to other bidders.

Ace was the new owner of ten, mostly mares. He and his family sat not far from Flynn, down a couple of rows and one section over. She'd noticed him glancing in her direction now and again, had noticed because her glance was constantly straying to him.

Enough already, she chided herself. *He's not worth it.*

And yet, her insides insisted on fluttering.

"What's taking so dang long?" her father complained to no one in particular.

"Are you going to bid on him?"

"Yep."

"A stud horse, Dad? What happened to retiring?"

"I wouldn't retire if I owned that horse."

He'd been going back and forth for months now. Flynn had, too.

If her father got out of the business and moved to Billings to be near her sister, what would she do?

She regularly helped with his bulls and string of bucking stock and had since she was a young girl. After earning her associate's degree in business administration, she also assisted him with the office work during evenings and weekends. Monday through Friday, she worked as an administrator at the Roundup Emergency Care Clinic. Pushing papers was her forte, if not her passion.

Once, she'd aspired to work in management for a large corporation. Except she hadn't been able to get her foot in the door. Not like her ex-husband, whose career had soared while hers stagnated.

They'd originally planned to wait a few years before starting a family. With her career stuck in neutral, Flynn saw no reason to postpone having the children she'd always wanted. Her ex-husband adamantly refused, and Flynn was forced to let another dream go unfulfilled.

Her discontent increased when her older sister, Nora, a pharmacist, married a great guy and promptly bore the first of Flynn's two nephews. How was it her sister seemed to effortlessly attain everything Flynn wanted?

If her father retired, there'd be opportunities. She'd been considering them for weeks with great deliberation. More since she lost her head and slept with Ace.

His abrupt departure had hurt, but it also drove home the point that the time had come and gone for her to let the past go and move forward.

The idea of returning to school appealed to her the most, but it would be next to impossible without moving from Roundup.

A rumbling from the crowd caused Flynn's head to snap up. Midnight was being led into the ring. No, *dragged* into the ring, by two wranglers. With all four hooves digging into the muddy dirt, the horse lowered his hindquarters almost to the ground and resisted the tug from the two lead ropes connected to his halter. A third man, the livestock foreman hired by Wally Dunlap's heirs, followed behind. He held a buggy whip and flicked it in the air behind Midnight, the snapping sound intended to encourage the horse.

It didn't. Midnight bore down harder.

Flynn wanted to shout a protest. She wasn't

alone. Ace sprang to his feet, an angry scowl on his face, his flyer crushed between his fingers.

Just when she thought he might leap across six bleacher rows and over the ring fence, the horse went suddenly still and straightened. The wranglers must have decided to quit while they were ahead because they abandoned their efforts and stood, the lead ropes stretched taut.

Midnight ignored them. Raising his head, he stared proudly and defiantly at the audience. His mane and forelock fluttered in the same chilly breeze that snuck up the back of Flynn's neck and caused her to shiver.

Or was the horse himself responsible for her reaction?

Up until this moment, she hadn't understood the fuss. Sure, Midnight was good-looking, with quality bloodlines and a proven history as a champion bucking horse and sire. But there were lots of stallions like him for sale these days.

Seeing Midnight in the ring, however, she glimpsed the greatness in him that had excited her father and Ace and everyone else at the auction.

"Isn't he something?"

"Are you sure about this, Dad?"

"I don't want Ace and Sarah to have him."

"Please don't turn this into a competition with them."

Her words fell on deaf ears. The auctioneer's singsong litany had started.

"What do you say? Let's start the bidding at twenty thousand dollars. Do I have twenty thousand?"

As if on cue, people inched forward in their seats, Flynn and her father included.

"Fifteen, do I hear fifteen?"

When the auctioneer dropped to five thousand dollars, the bidding took off. Her father didn't join in until the going price reached ten thousand dollars. Ace refrained, Flynn noticed, his attention riveted on the horse.

Her father's hand continually went up as he outbid everyone. When the price reached twenty-seven thousand dollars, only her father and one other man remained.

Flynn began to worry in earnest. Did her father have that kind of money?

"Twenty-seven, twenty-seven, someone give me twenty-eight thousand?" the auctioneer intoned.

"Twenty-seven, five."

Every head in the stands turned toward the sound of a new voice. It belonged to Ace.

"Dammit," Flynn's father groused beneath his breath and raised his hand again. "Twenty-eight."

"Twenty-nine." This from the other man.

With Ace's participation, the price was quickly driven up to thirty-five thousand dollars, her father making the last bid.

Flynn went from worrying to panicking. Surely he couldn't raise that much money. He was letting the excitement of the bidding cloud his judgment.

"Dad, don't be foolish."

"I want that horse."

"We'll buy another horse." A less expensive one.

"None of them are like Midnight."

Evidently Ace felt the same, for he shouted, "Thirty-six thousand dollars."

The other man promptly resigned with a discouraged head shake. "Too rich for my blood."

That left Ace and Flynn's father.

How was this possible? The two men she cared most for in the whole world were fighting over a stupid horse.

Wait a minute, she didn't care about Ace.

Right.

If someone ever invented a cure for unrequited love, she'd be the first in line to try it.

"Thirty-seven thousand," her father shouted.

The crowd clapped and cheered. Easy for them, Flynn thought, it wasn't their life's savings on the line.

"This is insane," she hissed. "You don't have thirty-seven thousand dollars."

"There's my line of credit with the bank."

"That's for running the business!"

"Buying a bucking horse is business."

"No, this is an absurd rivalry and refusing to let the Harts get one up on you. What's the matter with you? You don't act like this."

For a moment, time froze. Then his face fell, and he groaned miserably. "Oh, God. What's wrong with me?"

She reached for his hand and squeezed it between hers, relief leaving her weak.

"I don't know what came over me. It's just..." He groaned again.

"I have thirty-seven thousand dollars," the auctioneer boomed. "Do I have thirty-eight?"

Ace and his mother bent their heads together and conferred behind the shield of their hands.

"Going once."

Flynn went rigid. Why wasn't Ace bidding?

"Going twice."

Oh, no! What if the Harts dropped out?

Easy. Her father would have purchased a horse he really didn't need for a sum of money he couldn't possibly afford.

This couldn't be happening!

"Thirty-eight thousand," Ace shouted.

Flynn's heart started beating again.

When the auctioneer finally called, "Sold to number fifty-seven," a minute later, she let herself breathe.

The auction was over, and her father had spent no more than the price of gas for a round-trip.

Why, then, did he appear glum?

"Dad, you okay?" All around them the bleachers had started to empty, yet her father didn't rise.

"Yeah, sure."

"Is your indigestion bothering you again?"

"I'm fine." He promptly pushed to his feet and extended a hand to her. "Come on. Let's go home."

Flynn couldn't be more ready and happily dropped the subject of his health and listlessness. Maybe she'd phone her sister, Nora, tonight. See if she could convince their dad to open up about what was bothering him lately. Perhaps he was having a midlife crisis or had grown tired of being single all these years.

Grabbing two cups of coffee at the concession stand for the drive, she and her father strode across the area between the barn and the field that served as a parking lot. A line of people had formed in front of the converted motor home that was being used as a consignment office. The door to the motor home opened, and Ace and Sarah emerged. Ace went first, turning to assist his mother. They both wore happy smiles, Ace's devastatingly handsome.

Flynn ignored the quickening of her pulse. That smile had been her undoing once too often.

"Hold on a second." To her surprise, her father started toward the Harts.

"What is it?" She hurried after him.

Her question was answered when they met up with Ace and Sarah.

"Congratulations." Her father shook Sarah's hand, then Ace's. "You got yourself a fine stallion there."

Flynn sensed Ace studying her, and her

gloved fingers curled into tight balls. She would not return his look, not give him the satisfaction of learning the extent to which he affected her.

"Thank you, Earl." Sarah beamed. "I have to confess, he was almost yours."

"The right person bought him. Just wanted to tell you and that there are no hard feelings."

"I appreciate it. Truly, I do. Are you still considering adding to your string? There should be some quality livestock at the Miles City Sale."

"Naw. I'm going to quit the business."

Flynn exhaled. This time he sounded serious.

"What will you do?" Sarah asked.

"Sell off my string, the ranch, everything. Move to Billings to live near Nora and her husband."

"Oh, Earl. That's a big step."

"What are you going to do?" Ace asked.

It took Flynn a moment for her to realize he was speaking to her.

She did look at him then, unable to stop herself.

"Attend Montana State University," she said with newfound determination. "Enroll in nursing school."

"I didn't realize you wanted to be a nurse."

"For a while now." She glanced at her father. "I've been talking to some of the nurses at the clinic, and I think I'd be good at it."

Not that she didn't enjoy her job at the clinic—parts of it, anyway. But she was capable of so much more than grunt work. She wanted to have an impact. Make a difference. Contribute in a more meaningful way.

"You'll be a wonderful nurse." Sarah gave Flynn a brief but affectionate hug. "Earl, you must be proud."

"I'm proud of her whatever she does."

Flynn's triumph dimmed when she met Ace's frown.

Seriously? What did he have to be annoyed about?

"We're going to miss you," he said stiffly, and stuffed the sale papers he'd been holding into the front pocket of his jacket.

Your family, or you? Flynn wanted to ask, fairly certain she already knew the answer wasn't him.

Flynn was leaving! Moving to Billings. And she wanted to be a nurse. Ace couldn't believe it.

Not that she wouldn't make a great nurse,

he just didn't recall her ever mentioning it before.

Of course, the last time they were together, their talk had centered on their lovemaking and how incredible they made each other feel. Not any potential career changes.

"Heads-up!" Duke yelled.

The warning came in the nick of time. Ace jumped onto the bottom rung of the fence and out of the way a scant second before two of their newly purchased bucking mares trampled him. He remained clinging to the fence until the coast was clear, then hopped off.

"Three more to go," Uncle Joshua hollered from the pen. "Coming your way."

Ace's uncle lived on Thunder Ranch and was in charge of their remaining bulls and cattle. He'd moved to the ranch when his twin sons, Duke and Beau, were knee-high, as he was fond of saying. Before then, he'd spent many years working for Flynn's grandfather.

For supposed rivals, the Harts and the McKinleys were connected on many levels.

Ace's thoughts circled right back to Flynn. She was moving.

As much as he hated her leaving, it probably was for the best. She deserved a man able to commit to her, not one dividing himself between his vet practice and managing his family's various businesses.

"Pay attention," Duke complained.

"Sorry," Ace grumbled. "Got a lot on my mind."

They herded the remaining three horses down the narrow aisle and into the waiting stock trailer. Their hooves created a tremendous clatter as they hopped inside to join the other two horses, who shifted to accommodate the newcomers. A few squealed, defending their small territory against their neighbor.

While some bucking horses were friendly enough around people, others weren't. Driving them down a narrow aisle and up into a trailer was often the easiest and most effective method of loading them.

"Midnight the only one left?" Ace had been so preoccupied with Flynn, he'd lost track of the horses they'd already loaded. He glanced over at the second trailer they'd brought and started counting.

"The wranglers are bringing him round now," Duke said.

Ace didn't wait. He disliked the manner in which the wranglers and livestock foreman had handled Midnight during the auction.

Not that they'd hurt him, but they'd been un-necessarily heavy-handed.

While Duke and Uncle Joshua made sure the horses were secure for the trip, Ace trudged up the aisle to the pen holding Midnight. One wrangler held the horse's lead rope while the other manned the gate.

"Thanks for your help, guys," Ace told the wranglers. "I'll take it from here."

"Your horse." The wrangler at the gate stepped aside.

Ace went right up to Midnight and grabbed the lead rope from the second wrangler's outstretched hand. The rope went instantly slack. Well, well, Midnight was no longer fighting.

"Good boy," Ace crooned, stroking the horse's neck.

Midnight took a hesitant step toward the gate, then another.

"That's right." Ace walked along beside him, pleased Midnight was going to make this easy. He could use something going his way after his encounter with Flynn.

He and Midnight reached the gate. It was wide enough for only one of them to pass through at a time. Ace started to go first.

All at once, Midnight charged through the

gate, shoving Ace aside and into the railing. He tried but couldn't hang on to the lead rope and it tore from his grasp.

Free at last, the horse broke into a gallop.

"Look out," Ace yelled as Midnight bolted down the aisle.

Wranglers scrambled out of the horse's path, diving for cover. Ace ran after him, slipping and sliding in the muddy ground and nearly losing his balance twice. Pain sliced through his back from his collision with the railing.

When Midnight reached the end of the aisle, he skidded to a halt and stared at the trailer, his flanks heaving, his high-arched tail swishing nervously. Thank goodness the opening was blocked by the trailer, or else the horse would have likely made for the hills.

He swung his large body around as Ace approached, tossing his head angrily as if to say, "Drats, foiled again."

"Where exactly did you think you were going?" Ace stopped, bent, braced his hands on his knees and studied the horse, his lungs on fire.

Midnight pawed the ground, then turned back to face the trailer. A panel had been closed, separating the trailer into two compartments, the rear one empty. Ace could imagine the horse weighing his options.

"Make this easy, pal. Go in the trailer."

Duke and Uncle Joshua came over, their faces split by amused grins Ace didn't find the least bit funny. They'd exercised considerably more intelligence than him and remained on the opposite side of the fence railing, clear of harm's way.

"You should have seen yourself running after that horse." Uncle Joshua broke into laughter and elbowed Duke in the ribs. "Where's a video camera when you need one?"

Duke, usually more somber, laughed along with his dad.

"I just want to get this damn horse loaded," Ace grumbled.

Midnight snorted and pawed the ground again, his lead rope dangling in the mud.

"Need help?" the livestock foreman asked. He strolled toward Ace, the buggy whip gripped at his side.

"We're okay." In Ace's opinion, that livestock foreman and his whip were the reason Midnight bolted in the first place.

Raising his arms and waving them slowly,

Ace clucked to Midnight. The two wranglers came up behind Ace, blocking any potential escape route.

Duke started toward the slim opening between the fence and the rear corner of the trailer. "You want me to grab his lead rope?"

"No, stay put," Ace ordered. "The last thing we need is someone getting hurt."

Someone else getting hurt, he thought, and rolled his sore shoulder.

Five minutes later, Midnight had yet to budge.

"Aren't you supposed to be a horse whisperer?" the livestock foreman asked, a slight jeer in his voice. "Can't you just whisper him into the trailer?"

If only it were that simple.

Clouds gathered in the sky overhead, and the temperature had dropped by several degrees. It was going to rain again. Possibly snow. They really needed to be on the road soon to avoid any dangerous weather conditions.

Midnight stared at the trailer holding his companions. He wanted to be with them. Horses were herd animals by nature and this was his herd. But he was also stubborn and unwilling to give an inch.

"All of you, leave," Ace said.

"What?" Uncle Joshua scoffed. "You crazy?"

"You heard me. Leave." Ace turned to the wranglers and livestock foreman. "And no one comes round until that horse is loaded."

"I'm not leaving," Uncle Joshua protested.

"Come on, Dad." Duke clapped his father's shoulder. "Ace knows best."

The men shrugged and grumbled and complained, but they also did as requested. Ace was pretty sure he heard the livestock foreman refer to him by a rather colorful name.

Walking casually down the aisle, Ace left Midnight alone. He waited at the pen, keeping an eye on the horse. Unless Midnight chose to jump the five-foot fence, an unlikely probability, his options were limited.

"Let's go, boy," he muttered to himself. "Into the trailer. Nobody's watching you."

Midnight lifted one front leg, held it poised in the air.

Ace mentally willed the horse forward. "Come on, you can do it."

He noticed a few stragglers and the cleanup crew observing with obvious interest. His mother, too. He didn't care, as long as they stayed away.

A horse inside the trailer whinnied. Another one clanged a hoof against the sidewall.

It was apparently the encouragement Midnight needed. Tentatively, he approached the rear of the trailer. Placing one front foot on the trailer floor, he waited. And waited. Finally he hoisted the front half of his body inside.

"Halfway there, pal," Ace murmured.

With a mighty grunt, Midnight hopped into the trailer, settling himself in the empty compartment as if it were just another day, just another trailer ride.

Ace held up a warning hand to his cousin and uncle when they would have climbed the fence. He let a full minute pass before he started down the aisle. When he reached the trailer, he swung the rear gate closed and latched it, the metallic clink making a very satisfying sound.

"Hallelujah!" Uncle Joshua exclaimed. "Let's get the heck out of here before the storm hits."

Ace checked Midnight one last time, chuckling to himself. He was going to like this horse.

Chapter 3

Ace and Duke climbed into the cab of the truck hauling Midnight and the mares. His mother and uncle got into the cab of the other truck. They formed a small caravan as they slowly navigated the road from the auction grounds to Highway 12.

"You hungry?" Duke asked.

"Starving." Waiting out stubborn horses was hard work, as was an unplanned confrontation with an irate woman.

"I'll call Dad in a bit. Maybe we can eat at the truck stop we passed on the way here."

Ace removed his cowboy hat and set it on the seat between him and Duke. By prior agreement, they'd split the chore of driving. Ace had taken the first shift to the auction from Roundup, needing the distraction to combat his nervousness.

He wished he was driving now, he could use another distraction. When he wasn't contemplating Midnight's puzzling behavior, he was imagining Flynn packing boxes and cartons in preparation for moving. She'd been a fixture in his life for much of it, except during the time she was married.

He'd never liked her husband and was convinced the fool didn't deserve Flynn.

Ace didn't deserve her, either.

He recalled her face that morning three weeks ago and grimaced. Could he have treated her more cruelly? He'd told himself it was necessary, that to lead her on would be unfair. She'd form expectations, ones he couldn't meet.

The truth was he'd been running scared, that morning and every day since. Even before they'd gone to her house, before their first kiss outside the Number 1 Diner, something inside him had changed. He finally admitted to himself that Flynn was someone he could easily fall for, had, in all likelihood, fallen for years earlier and simply denied it.

"Some news about Flynn going to school to be a nurse." Duke glanced at the side mirrors before changing lanes.

"Who told you?"

"Your mom. She's worried."

"About Flynn? Why?"

"No, about you. She said you took it pretty hard."

"Why would I take it hard? I think it's a great idea." Ace shoved his fingers through his hair, wiping the sweat from his brow. "Want me to call your dad? The truck stop's coming up soon."

"Not for half an hour."

Ace didn't want to discuss Flynn. He hadn't told anyone about the night they'd spent together and wouldn't. Not even Duke. And they were more than cousins, they were good friends.

In some ways, Ace had a better relationship with Duke than he did with his own brothers. Colt was frequently off to some rodeo and Tuf had enlisted in the Marines. On the other hand, Ace and Dinah were close. She was the little sister he ordered around, doted on, protected, and whose secrets he safeguarded.

His gut clenched at the reminder. Flynn

and Dinah talked on a regular basis. Had she confided in Dinah about her and Ace? It was possible.

"I don't know why your mom's worried," Duke said thoughtfully. "For a while there we all thought you and Flynn were going to hook up."

"That was years ago." Duke was one of the few people who knew Ace and Flynn had dated.

"I'm talking last month." Duke slanted Ace a bemused smile. "We saw you and her leaving the Number 1."

Ace abruptly sat up, then slumped against the seat, afraid of giving himself away. "We?"

"Dad, Beau and I."

Both his cousins *and* his uncle?

"Royce, Harlan and Gracie were there, too."

Three of the Harts' ranch hands? Great. Ace and Flynn might as well have taken an ad out in the *Roundup Record Tribune.*

"I don't want to talk about it." Which was not the same as saying nothing happened, and Duke probably picked up on the subtle difference.

"Your business."

Duke respected Ace's wishes for the remainder of the drive to Thunder Ranch, avoiding the topic of Flynn and Ace even when his mother brought Flynn up over dinner at the truck stop.

Ace was never so glad to see the exit for home.

They drove the mile-long driveway into Thunder Ranch, past the main house with its rustic charm and fieldstone wall to the various outbuildings, one of them a newly constructed mare motel. Luckily they beat the snow, which started falling in earnest the minute they pulled up in front of the horse barn.

"It's too late and too cold." Ace reached behind the seat and retrieved his and Duke's yellow all-weather ponchos. "Let's just put the mares and geldings in the west paddock for tonight. We can move them tomorrow if there's a break in the weather."

"And Midnight?"

"The clinic."

Ace had constructed a pair of shaded corrals behind the horse barn, which also contained a small office he used for his vet practice. The corrals were for quarantining sick or injured animals while he treated them. It wasn't an ideal location for Midnight, but it would suffice until the construction of his stud quarters was completed.

Duke braked to a stop, letting Ace out long enough to dash through the snow and relay their plans to his uncle in the other truck.

"Meet you at the paddock with the rest of the horses once we've unloaded Midnight," he told his uncle.

"You going to need some help?"

"We can handle it."

Ace returned to the truck. Midnight, impatient to get out, had begun kicking the trailer wall. He was still creating a ruckus while Duke backed the trailer to the corral gate. If all went as intended, the horse would go right from the trailer to the corral without incident.

Turning on an overhead floodlight, Ace positioned himself at the trailer door. Duke reached through the open slats and unfastened Midnight's lead rope from where it was tied.

The horse stood perfectly still.

Ace wasn't fooled. When he sensed the moment was right, he opened the trailer door.

"Welcome home, boy."

The horse flicked his ears and cranked his

big head around, calmly assessing his new surroundings.

"I think he'll be okay," Ace told Duke confidently after several uneventful seconds. "Now that we're away from the auction and that livestock foreman."

"Yeah, okay. If you say so."

Before Ace could reply, Midnight flung himself sideways out of the trailer, landing with a wet thud on the ground. Ace and Duke tripped over their feet attempting to escape danger. Midnight catapulted into the corral. Running and bucking—oh, man, could that horse buck—he circled the corral a few times before coming to a stop.

"Duke! Are you all right?" Ace slammed the corral gate shut, then ran to his cousin, who leaned awkwardly against the trailer wheel well.

"I'm fine." He cradled his left elbow close to his body.

"Here." Ace gripped his cousin's forearm and gently manipulated the affected joint. "Does that hurt?"

"Hell, yes."

"Hurt like you fractured it?"

"Naw. Nothing a little ice, aspirin and a cold beer won't fix."

"Sorry about that."

"Not your fault. Is Midnight okay?"

"Him? That horse is made of solid steel. You going to be able to work tomorrow?"

"Shoot, I'm tougher than that." Duke served part-time as one of Roundup's deputies under the recently elected sheriff—none other than Ace's sister, Dinah. "It's you I'm worried about."

"I didn't get hurt."

"I mean your investment." He hitched his chin at the corral. "You and your mom have a lot on the line."

They did. Ace believed in his mother's vision, which was that a secure future lay in their bucking stock contracting operation. To that end, she'd taken out a three-hundred thousand dollar loan, which he'd cosigned.

If they didn't succeed, Ace could potentially lose his vet practice.

He'd worked too hard, sacrificed too much, for that to happen.

"I'll drive the mares to the paddock," he said.

"Forget it. I'll meet Dad with the mares. You stay here and settle Midnight in."

"Are you positive?"

Duke's response was to head for the cab of the truck.

Ace shut the trailer door. After his cousin drove off, he retrieved two flakes of hay from the small stack he kept by the corral and tossed them in the feeder. Midnight started eating immediately, happy as a pig with his slop.

"I should have counted on you doing something crazy," Ace muttered, disappointed with himself. When it came to horses, his instincts were usually right on the mark.

Midnight stopped eating long enough to give Ace a you-just-met-your-match look.

Yeah, he had.

Most stallions were unpredictable to some degree, as were many bucking horses. Midnight, as Ace was quickly realizing, verged on unmanageable.

What had happened to this fine animal in the past two years to so dramatically alter his personality?

Duke wasn't the only one worried. Ace couldn't help wondering if he and his mother had made a mistake, paid a small fortune in a stud horse they couldn't handle and didn't dare put with their mares on the chance he'd injure them.

* * *

Flynn stared at the pregnancy test wand. Just how reliable were these things?

Pretty accurate, she knew from working at the emergency clinic.

She could always go to the clinic, have the doctor administer a second test in order to confirm, but why? Her body had been telling her for days what the test wand in her hand confirmed: Flynn was having a baby.

She'd become, she realized with a sigh, a statistic. One night of lovemaking, and she'd gotten pregnant. What were the odds?

Considerably greater than with a couple who actually practiced birth control.

Flynn was no idiot; heck, she worked in the medical profession and witnessed the results of unprotected sex on a weekly basis. She could offer excuses. More than once she'd forgotten to take her birth control pill and hadn't gotten pregnant. Her night with Ace had been spontaneous and they were caught unprepared. According to her cycle, it was a safe time of the month.

She moaned softly.

The fact was they'd both acted irresponsibly, and Flynn held the consequences in her hand.

No, carried them inside her. Setting the wand on the bathroom sink, she pressed a palm to her belly.

A baby! The timing couldn't be any worse and, my goodness, what would Ace say?

She slipped the wand into her robe pocket and inspected herself in the bathroom mirror, tilting her head to the side. She was going to be a mother in, she mentally counted, about eight months! Thanksgiving time.

Did she look any different?

What had her own mother thought when she realized she was carrying Flynn's older sister, Nora?

That a baby was the last thing she wanted?

Flynn considered calling Dinah, asking her friend to meet her after work. Flynn could use an ear to bend, a shoulder to lean on. But Dinah was Ace's sister and the two of them were thick as thieves. Flynn couldn't chance Ace finding out about the baby until she was ready to tell him. Until she'd decided on a course of action.

She'd have the baby, there was no question of that. With the possible exception of Ace, she hadn't wanted anything more. Ever. Her way of compensating for her mother's abandonment, she supposed, and Paul's. His refusal to even consider having children for years and years into the future had been the final, backbreaking straw in their shaky marriage, ending with him walking out on her.

A baby. She still couldn't believe it! The prospect petrified her. Wanting children didn't necessarily mean she was ready to be a mother. It also thrilled her. This was a dream come true.

Flynn stumbled from the bathroom, the news of her condition, more than the condition itself, making her light-headed. She usually awoke after her father, so it was no surprise to find him in the kitchen, drinking a cup of coffee, nibbling on a piece of toast and reviewing paperwork.

"Morning, sweetie pie." His tone lacked his usual enthusiasm and his smile its usual luster.

Who was she kidding? Her father's smile had been mostly lusterless for months.

How to tell him about the baby? She longed to share her news with someone who loved and understood her. Dinah was out of the question and Nora, the next logical choice, would be in the middle of dropping her sons off at day care on her way to work. Forget calling her mother. Flynn wasn't in the mood for a lecture.

She reached for the pot of coffee on the counter, then stopped. Returning the mug to the cupboard, she grabbed a juice glass instead. Caffeine wasn't good for the baby. Orange juice, however, very good.

"What are you looking at, Dad?"

"This is a listing agreement with the real estate agent I hired."

"Really?" She sat at the table. "When did you talk to him?"

"Her. And it was yesterday. We met while you were at work."

Well, he'd certainly moved quickly. He'd only just announced to the Harts on Saturday he was selling everything and getting out of the business. Today was Tuesday.

"Are you going to sign it?"

"Already did." He held up the agreement for her to see. "Just reviewing it and making notes."

"Wow." Flynn's throat inexplicably tightened. This wasn't the first time she'd moved from Roundup. Why, then, were her emotions threatening to spill over?

Must be the baby and hormones.

"Sweetie pie, what's wrong?"

Flynn glanced up to find her dad studying her. "Nothing. Actually, everything's falling into place perfectly. You're selling the ranch, we're moving to Billings, I'm going to nursing school."

"Then why are you crying?"

She touched her cheek, stunned to find it damp.

What a mess. Everything wasn't perfect.

Having a baby was supposed to be exhilarating. Deeply satisfying. One of life's greatest joys. Flynn felt those things. She was also still in shock and uncertain. At this moment, those feelings overwhelmed the others.

"Dad," she blurted. "I have something to tell you. You're going to be surprised. A good surprise, I hope."

Please let him be happy for me.

He laid the listing agreement aside, his expression concerned. "You're not going back to school?"

She could do both, right? Go to school and have a baby?

"No. I am." She swallowed. This was much harder than she'd anticipated. "I'm… Wow." She gathered her wildly racing thoughts. "I'm pregnant."

He sat back, his eyes wide and unblinking. "That *is* a surprise."

"I only found out myself a few minutes ago when I took the home pregnancy test."

"How far along are you?" he stammered.

"A month or so."

Flynn's chest tightened, and her eyes stung. She wished her father would stop sitting there, staring at her. "You're disappointed in me."

"God, no, Flynn." He sprang from his chair, hauled her to her feet and clasped her to him. "I love you, I could never be disappointed in you. It's just like you say, a surprise." He set her back from him, brushed her hair from her face in a familiar and tender gesture reminiscent of when she was a young girl. "I love being a grandfather. It's one of the reasons I want to move to Billings. And I know how much you've always hankered for kids of your own. I just figured…"

"That I'd be married."

"Something like that. I'm your old man." He shrugged apologetically. "Can't help wanting what I think is best for you."

Flynn hugged him fiercely, laid her head on his chest.

"I'm happy for you, sweetie pie."

"I'm happy, too. And a little nervous."

"Kids are a big step." He kissed the top of her head. "But you'll do fine. And you'll be a wonderful mother." He grew suddenly serious. "You are keeping the baby."

"Of course I am!"

"That's good." He patted her reassuringly. "Is Ace the dad?"

Now it was Flynn's turn to stare at her father in confusion. "H-how did you—"

"Because, there really hasn't been any other man for you."

If her father knew, then chances were Sarah Hart did, too. All those months trying to hide her and Ace's relationship from their parents had apparently been for nothing.

Flynn grimaced. What would Ace's mother, his whole family, think of her when they found out about the baby?

"Do you love him?" her father asked.

Flynn involuntarily stiffened. Dinah Hart had been the only one to ask her that before. She'd noticed Flynn's crush on her older brother, a crush that had developed into much more when she and Ace dated.

Except Flynn had kept those feelings hidden and always would, not even telling Dinah.

"I— I'm… It's complicated."

Thankfully her father didn't pressure her for more. They returned to their chairs, and he clasped her hand across the table. "I take it you haven't told Ace yet."

"No."

"Are you going to?"

Flynn pushed her half-empty juice glass away. It suddenly didn't appeal to her anymore. "I wouldn't hide the baby from him. But I'm going to wait until I visit the obstetrician. Make sure everything's okay."

"Well, you could have picked a worse guy."

"Dad!"

"I meant that as a compliment. I've always liked Ace. It was John Hart I had a problem with. The man drank like a fish and practically ran his ranch into the ground before he died."

"That's harsh."

"Well, he did. But I have nothing other than respect for Sarah and Ace. He's ten times the man his father was. All them kids are, in their own way. But Ace most of all. He stepped up. Took over as head of the family. Runs the ranch with his mother. Hell of a vet, too. He'll make a good dad."

"I don't think Ace would agree with you

about his father. He and John may have butted heads, but Ace loved him. After John died, Ace took over because he thought it was what his father would have wanted."

In her mind, Flynn could hear Ace telling her those exact words ten years ago when he ended their brief dating relationship.

"Like I said, he's a better man than his father. He's trying to make something of that ranch, and not just for himself. Nothing he wouldn't sacrifice for his family. Nothing he wouldn't sacrifice for you and your baby, too."

"You're probably right."

"He'll insist on doing the right thing."

"I'm not getting married, if that's what you're implying." Flynn shocked herself with her vehemence.

"Why not?"

"Come on, Dad. I already have one disastrous marriage under my belt."

"You didn't love Paul."

Just how much had her father observed? She'd evidently underestimated him for years.

"I did love him." Not like she had—did— Ace. "In the beginning. We…" She hesitated, her voice thickening. These emotional highs and lows simply had to stop. "We drifted apart."

"He ignored you."

"Not always."

"Almost always." Her father snorted. "More interested in his job than you."

Paul's ambition was a quality Flynn had liked and admired when they first met. She hadn't foreseen that his ambition would one day consume him. After a few years, it became obvious he knew his coworkers more intimately than he did Flynn and shared more with them. She grew to resent that same ambition she'd once admired and the endless hours he put in at the office.

"He wasn't the only one at fault. I made my share of mistakes. I let him walk all over me instead of putting my foot down."

Her father snorted again, his way of saying his girls were perfect.

Flynn smiled despite her weepiness. He may think she had nothing to do with her failed marriage, but Flynn knew better. She'd made mistakes, the first one being rushing to the altar.

She'd met Paul in one of her classes at community college; they hit it off and got engaged shortly after graduating. Flynn had assumed their similar career goals—to advance, to climb the corporate ladder—would bind them. She hadn't anticipated their differences when it came to starting a family.

Flynn had asked him for a separation, hoping the shock would shake up Paul and force him to admit how much he loved her and wanted to stay married.

Only, what he'd said was, "Why bother with a separation? Let's just get a divorce." He'd packed up his belongings and left the next day.

"I'm not going to make any rash decisions," Flynn announced resolutely. "This baby is too important to me."

"Too bad about nursing school," her father said. "You'd have made a good nurse."

Flynn straightened. "I can still go to school. I'll start the enrollment process now. Take online classes until after the baby's born."

She was going to be a mother. A single mother. Now more than ever she needed a decent job with security and benefits and potential for advancement.

"That's an awful lot to have going on at once. Especially if you're working, too."

She would need to keep working. She couldn't afford to pay for school otherwise.

Her temples began to throb. There was so much to think about.

"I'll start slow. One or two classes."

"Hmm," her father mumbled in a tone that implied maybe Flynn should reconsider. "What about Ace? He's going to want to be a dad to your child."

"And he can be. Visit as much as he wants. Billings is only an hour away from here."

Her father chuckled and raised his coffee mug in a toast. "Good luck with that."

"What?" Flynn made a face. "I'll be generous."

"We're talking about Ace Hart. The man isn't going to want you to go anywhere, not with his child. He's going to fight you tooth and nail and we both know it."

Flynn hated it when her father was right.

Chapter 4

Ace fished his keys from his jeans pocket as he headed out of the barn.

Flynn had called that morning requesting he meet her at the old fishing hole on Thunder Creek when they were both off work. He'd agreed without hesitation, assuming she was giving him the chance to make good on the apology he owed her.

Now that he was about to see her, doubts crept in.

There'd been an unusual nervous quality in her voice. He hadn't heard anything like it in ten years, not since he'd asked to meet her at the same fishing hole. His father had recently died, and Ace had informed Flynn it was over between them.

His thoughts returned to the auction five days ago. She hadn't been nervous then.

Could she have changed her mind about moving and going to nursing school?

Even if she had, she wouldn't insist on a private meeting in a secluded spot to inform him. There had to be another reason.

Like giving him the chewing out he richly deserved without any prying ears nearby.

He was about to start the engine when Gracie came running from the barn to his truck, one hand securing her hat to her head, the other one clutching a piece of paper. The single mother and only female ranch hand had worked for the Harts two years this coming May. She took a lot of flack from the men and repaid them by dishing out an equal amount, which earned her their respect. Ace liked her, too.

He lowered the driver's side window, letting in a blast of cold air. Thunder Creek probably wasn't the best meeting place.

"What's wrong?"

"The blood work on Midnight just came in from the lab," Gracie said in a huff when she reached the truck. "I thought you'd want to see it before you left."

Ace grabbed the sheet of paper and quickly scanned it, his heart hammering.

He hoped to discover a cause for Midnight's unruly disposition and aversion to people. In an attempt to eliminate any underlying medical reason, he'd put the horse through a battery of health tests, which only made him distrust Ace even more.

"Bad news?" Gracie had assisted Ace during the exams and had taken an interest in Midnight.

"No, good news." Actually, the results couldn't be any better. Like every other test Ace had conducted. "Everything's normal."

Which meant the horse's behavior problems were the result of his genetic makeup, social environment or handling.

His *recent* handling, Ace thought, distaste filling his mouth. Midnight had successfully competed in rodeos for years before Wally Dunlap became ill and turned over the management of his string to a hired foreman. The only reputation Midnight had earned before that was giving cowboys record-breaking rides and producing superior quality offspring.

What had happened to trigger such a dramatic change in him?

Ace was determined to find out.

"Thanks, Gracie." He handed the paper back to her. "Can you put that on my desk for me? I'm going to—" He paused. Gracie had been one of the people to see him and Flynn at the diner last month. "I'll be back later tonight."

"Sure thing, boss. Oh, and I forgot. Colt gave me a message for you. He left for the PRCA Championship Rodeo in Fargo and will be home on Monday."

Ace's fingers choked the steering wheel. He stopped squeezing only when he noticed Gracie's gaze cutting to his hands.

When was his brother going to grow up, quit playing and do something more around the ranch than the least amount of work he could get away with?

No, that would make things easier on Ace, and Colt was all about himself.

"See you in the morning." Ace started the engine. "Call me if there's a problem with Midnight."

Grace hurried off in the direction of the barn and Ace's office.

He drove away, his focus changing from his brother to Flynn and their meeting.

The road to the old fishing spot was

bumpy and winding and overgrown. Piles of unmelted snow and soggy patches made the driving treacherous. Ace hoped Flynn had borrowed her father's truck and not brought her compact car.

She was already waiting for him when he arrived—her father's pickup parked with its left front wheel resting on an incline. The roar of furiously rushing water filled his ears as he picked his way down the slope. Barren brush snagged his pant legs. Come summer, when the snow had long melted, the river would once again flow lazily and the woods be overgrown with thick, lush greenery.

Flynn sat near the bank on the trunk of an overturned pine tree, a recent casualty of their hard winter. She held her spine rigid, as if bracing for the worst. Did the prospect of seeing him fill her with that much dread?

For the thousandth time, he wished he could return to that morning weeks ago.

"Hi." He spoke softly so as not to startle her, though she'd surely heard his boots crushing twigs and scraping across rough ground.

She swiveled to face him, watching him descend the last few feet. "Hi." She smiled weakly. "Thanks for coming."

He lowered himself onto the tree trunk beside her, choosing it over the boulder which sat twelve feet away. Their thighs brushed momentarily before she scooted sideways to accommodate him, but not before a rush of heat shot through him.

"You okay?" he asked, curious if she felt the same heat.

"Fine." She held her clasped hands in her lap, their pale color matching her cheeks.

No heat rushing through her.

"Flynn, whatever you need. I'm here for you."

"This is difficult." She swallowed. Fidgeted. "I really hope you're not angry with me."

"There's nothing you can do to make me mad."

"You say that now."

"If anything, you should be mad at me. I'm really sorry for the way I bailed on you. There was no excuse for it." Not a good excuse, leastwise. Losing his nerve was a poor reason if Ace had ever heard one. "I can't tell you how much I regret it. The leaving. Not… the night. Us."

He needed to shut his mouth before he said something more stupid than he already had.

She exhaled a shallow, thready breath. "You're not making this easy."

"Just tell me. What's wrong?"

She stared at the river with its pockets of foaming white water.

Was she, like him, remembering all the times they'd come here when they were dating? They'd fish for hours without talking much. If the evenings were especially sultry and the stars out in abundance, they made love.

"I really wish things were different," he said, his fingers inching toward hers. "That I didn't have so much going on."

She stiffened. "Or, what? You'd ask me out?"

"Yeah, I would."

"I'm pregnant."

Ace's hand went still, then fell to his side. "Wow."

"It was an accident. I didn't plan it. You have to believe me."

"I do." Their night together had been as spontaneous as it was amazing. "We failed to use birth control. It's my fault more than yours."

Of all the times in Ace's life for him to slip up and be irresponsible.

Look what happened. Flynn was pregnant.

Ace concentrated on breathing, on forcing air into his collapsed lungs.

"I went to the doctor yesterday," she said. "She told me everything's fine. Progressing right on schedule."

"That's good."

"You're upset."

"I'm surprised is all. Give me a minute."

He'd always wanted children. It had been a frequent topic during their long-ago fishing trips. Just not yet. Later, when his vet practice was established and the new breeding business was running smoothly. When he didn't have a quarter-of-a-million-dollar loan hanging over his head.

"I realize the timing isn't great."

Flynn had been reading his mind.

"I'll support you and the baby in every way. Financially. Emotionally."

"I'm going to apply for a student grant. That should—"

"You're not still moving to Billings?"

"My plans haven't changed."

"Well, they need to change. This is my baby, too."

"I realize that family is important to you. How could I not?"

She was referring to when they broke up ten years ago.

"After my dad died, I didn't have any choice. I needed to finish school and help Mom run the ranch. There wasn't anybody else to do it."

"So you said. Countless times."

"Tuf joined the Marines. Dinah was trying to turn her life around. Colt decided he'd rather be on the road than at home. What was I supposed to do?"

"Exactly what you did."

"We were nearly broke, thanks to my dad."

A surge of anger from years earlier resurfaced, stifling Ace. How could his father have been so careless with the ranch?

Easy. Alcohol had clouded his judgment.

"You're right, your mom needed you." Flynn rubbed her temples. "I didn't mean to dredge up the past."

"I want to be an active father. Change diapers. Take the 3:00 a.m. feeding. Rock him or her to sleep." Ace wasn't sure where this spontaneous paternal drive came from, only that the baby mattered greatly. "I can't do those things if you're in Billings."

"Like you said, you have an awful lot on your plate right now."

"This is my child. You have to stay."

"Billings isn't far. You can visit. Often."

"I'm not driving an hour to see my child."

"Once Dad sells the ranch and moves, there's nothing keeping me here."

Was he nothing?

Apparently so.

"What about your job?"

"I'm enrolling in nursing school."

"Won't that be an awful lot on *your* plate? School and taking care of a baby?"

"I can manage. Between my dad and my sister and day care."

"Day care?" He scowled. "You'd let strangers take care of our child?"

"I'll find qualified day care. The university may have a facility."

"No."

She gaped at him, her jaw slack. "I beg your pardon?"

"I don't want you leaving our baby in day care. There has to be another solution."

"Like what? You watch him?"

"Why not? He could stay here with me during the week and you have him on the weekends. My mom will help." As if she wasn't as busy as Ace.

"No way!"

"You don't get to make all the decisions, Flynn."

Her mouth quivered. "Neither do you."

Ace paused, breathed deeply. He hated being harsh with her. "It's only late March. You won't be starting school until, what? The fall?"

"I was hoping to take some online classes this summer."

"You can do that from here."

"And Billings."

"Not until your dad's ranch sells, which gives us a little time to decide. Together."

She shrugged.

"Flynn." He took a chance, reached out and captured her hand. "We're having a baby. It's pretty incredible when you think about it."

She wiped at the tears spilling from her eyes.

"Don't cry." He'd always been a sucker for a woman's tears and ached to kiss her.

Better not. She'd probably club him up the side of the head.

A hug, that was the safer option.

He put an arm around her, pulled her close and stroked her back. "It's going to be okay. *We're* going to be okay."

She surprised him by returning the hug and burying her face in his jacket.

He cupped the back of her neck, threaded his fingers into the hair that had escaped her colorful stocking cap.

"There's another solution, you know," he murmured.

"What's that?"

"We get married."

She pushed away from him. "Ace, I can't."

"Won't you at least consider it?"

"No."

Her quick and adamant rejection stung.

Was the prospect of marrying him really that intolerable?

"Ace, I'm sorry. That came out wrong." Flynn rose from the log and joined Ace at the creek bank where he stood watching the water rush past. "I wasn't expecting you to propose. It really was a sweet gesture."

"Sweet?" He looked crushed.

"Okay, that came out wrong, too."

"Flynn, I'm serious. I want to marry you."

"I know you're serious. And, honestly, that's what scares me."

"Because of your divorce?"

"Marriage is a big commitment. Hopefully, a lifetime commitment. Take it from me, marrying for the wrong reasons can lead to a lot of unhappiness."

"A child seems like a pretty good reason to me."

She softened her voice. "You only proposed because you don't want me to move."

"That hit below the belt."

"Maybe, but it's true."

"How do you know?"

"Let's be honest. You don't have feelings for me—"

"I do. Couldn't you tell from our night together?"

"All right, then, what kind of feelings?"

"I care about you," he replied, a tad too defensively.

What had she expected? A flowery declaration? "I made a promise to myself after my divorce. I'm not going to marry any man who doesn't love me."

"Your ex-husband didn't love you?"

"Not enough to make our marriage work. The same with my parents. You know my mom walked out on us when I was young. What you don't know is Paul did the same thing to me."

Ace remained silent for several seconds.

Several very telling seconds. When he finally spoke, it was haltingly. "The other night, it wasn't just the sex. I haven't been that close to anyone before."

Looking away was impossible and, boy, did Flynn try. "For me, either."

They'd been intimate a few times when they dated in college. Here at this very spot, in fact. But Flynn had been completely inexperienced and Ace not much more. Ten years had brought about a lot of changes, for both of them.

Ace's skill as a lover had been matched only by his emotional intensity. He wasn't always as strong and confident and capable as he wanted people to think. Sometimes he let his guard down.

He had that night, allowing her to see a vulnerable side of him he mostly kept hidden.

And she'd fallen a little more in love.

"There isn't anyone else I'd want for the father of my baby," she admitted. "You'll be a good one, I'm sure of it."

"Then give us a chance."

"I told you—"

"Not to get married. I realize I'm rushing you. But to be the best parents we can. Raise our child together."

She did owe him that much. "You're right. We have time. I won't be moving for a while."

"I'm not going to change my mind. I want you and the baby living close to me."

Flynn should have heeded her father's advice more closely when he'd warned her about Ace's determination.

"Are you going to tell your family?" she asked.

"Soon. Once I figure out what I'm going to say." He smiled crookedly.

Flynn turned away from that charming smile to stare at the sun descending toward the distant mountaintops.

"What's wrong?" Ace touched her shoulder.

"I'm worried about what they'll think of me."

"Mom will be overjoyed. She doesn't understand how she could raise four kids to adulthood and none of them make her a grandmother yet."

"I can see your mom being happy."

"And she likes you."

"I like her, too." Flynn couldn't picture a better, kinder grandmother than Sarah Hart.

Then again, almost anyone would be a better grandmother than Flynn's own mother.

"Have you told your parents yet?" Ace asked.

"My dad."

"And?"

"He's pretty excited. He adores Nora's two sons."

"What about your mom?"

He would have to mention her mother.

Flynn sniffed. "I haven't spoken to her since last Christmas."

Her contact with her mother was infrequent and that suited her fine. For some reason, Nora had fewer painful memories of their childhood than Flynn and could talk to their mother without resentment rising up to choke her.

"Are you going to tell her?" Ace asked.

"Maybe. If I don't, Nora will."

Flynn's gaze returned to the sunset. "My mother wasn't what you'd call a good role model."

"You're not like her, Flynn."

"Am I that easy to read?"

"You forget, I know you."

Not like he thought he did or he'd see the love she carried around for him in her heart.

A painful lump in the back of her throat made speaking difficult. "I would never abandon my children for anyone or anything. Ever."

"Neither would I. You and our baby are stuck with me for the long haul."

She believed him. The Harts were close-knit, and Ace unerringly loyal.

That loyalty also scared her. He may not abandon her or their child, but he wouldn't give as much of himself as Flynn needed. The family business and his vet practice would come first. It had before, it would again.

She shivered as a breeze swept over them. "We should probably head home. I don't want to drive that road in the dark."

He helped her to climb the slope, held her hand until she found her footing.

"I'll call you tomorrow," he said at the top where their trucks were parked.

The words hung between them. If only he'd told her that a month ago, their conversation today might have gone differently. She'd still be pregnant, but she wouldn't have so many doubts about his motives.

"All right. Evening is better. I'm working the day shift at the clinic this week."

He walked her to her father's truck and opened the door. Before she could climb in, he circled her waist and drew her close. It was nice to be held by a pair of strong, muscular arms, and Flynn let herself melt into his embrace. For a moment, she could almost believe everything was going to be all right.

How could she be mad at him for proposing and for wanting her to stay in Roundup? He might have had an entirely different reaction to her announcement. Told her the baby was her problem and refused any responsibility whatsoever.

Ace no sooner released her than her sense of security faded, leaving Flynn feeling alone and more than a little scared about what lay ahead.

Chapter 5

Ace liked starting every morning with a plan. Today, he intended to make headway with Midnight, somehow, someway. If he couldn't discover what lay at the root of the horse's unmanageableness and resolve the issue, he'd settle for behavior modification.

He gave himself one month.

If, at the end of that time, Midnight didn't make measurable progress, Ace was going to recommend to his mother they sell him at the Miles City Bucking Horse Sale, take their losses and acquire a new stud.

Second on his list for the day was breaking the news to his family about Flynn's pregnancy.

He'd kept the news to himself for several days, wanting to process the ramifications first. He still hadn't decided between one big announcement at dinner or approaching each family member individually.

Their reactions didn't worry him, he honestly believed they'd be thrilled for him and Flynn. There would be questions, however. Probing ones. He might grow less tired answering them all at once.

Carrying his favorite saddle to the pens behind the barn, he hoisted it onto the fence railing. Midnight tracked Ace's every move, ears pricked forward, eyes alert. Ace made a second trip to the tack room, returning with a bucket of water, a sponge and a container of saddle soap. He also brought along a half-dozen carrots.

Setting the cleaning supplies on the ground, he opened the swinging panel in order to form a single large pen.

Midnight huffed and remained resolutely on his side, guarding his territory.

Ace set about cleaning his saddle, all the while maintaining a quiet conversation with the horse.

"I treated an old donkey at Angie Barrington's animal rescue this morning. The darn thing had the worst eye infection I've ever seen. He'll be lucky if he doesn't lose his sight."

Midnight wasn't interested. His attention had started to wander to the mares and yearlings in the distant pasture.

After a few more minutes, a few more scrubbings on the saddle and a few more casual observations about his morning rounds, Ace removed his jacket and hung it on a fence post. The weather wasn't quite warm enough to forego outerwear, but he'd make do. Picking up the carrots he'd brought, he shoved three in each of his back pockets.

Fifteen feet wasn't so far away Midnight couldn't smell a treat, and he instantly honed in on the carrots.

Ace resumed nonchalantly cleaning the saddle. He could practically hear the horse's nostrils quivering. At one point, Midnight advanced a step closer, his hooves scuffling on the hard ground. Ace didn't turn around, just kept cleaning the saddle. With any luck, Midnight would venture near enough to snatch the carrots from Ace's pockets.

He was prepared to wait, the entire afternoon if necessary. Of course he might have the cleanest saddle on the whole ranch.

After another ten minutes, Midnight had crept inch by inch to about ten feet away, his head bobbing with frustration. He wanted those carrots.

All at once, he emitted a loud squeal and scrambled to the far side of the pen, hind legs kicking.

Ace looked up and spotted his brother Colt ambling toward him.

Just when Ace was getting somewhere.

He flung the sponge into the bucket, creating a small splash.

"What's up?" Colt asked, completely indifferent to Ace's irritation.

"I was working with Midnight. Until you scared him."

"I did? Sorry."

"Dammit, Colt. I gave strict instructions. I wasn't to be disturbed."

"You need a hand?" Colt rested his forearms on the fence beside Ace's saddle, clearly not receiving the message to leave any more than he had Ace's original instructions.

"Are you kidding?"

The only reason Ace didn't get angrier with his brother was because of Midnight. The horse watched them warily from the farthest corner of the pen. A shouting match would only spook him and make him even more afraid of Ace.

That, and losing his cool with Colt would do no good. His brother was immune, wrapped up in his own world most of the time.

"I said I was sorry."

Ace exhaled, reined in his temper. "It's going slowly. I'm more and more convinced the livestock foreman mistreated Midnight and probably the other horses, as well."

Colt shook his head. "I don't get people like him."

It was one of the few things Ace and his brother had in common. Mostly they were a study in contradictions, appearance *and* personalitywise. Strangers might not even recognize them as being related. Ace had inherited their father's six-foot-plus height and dark looks. Colt, with his blond hair, green eyes and boyish, devil-may-care smile, resembled their mother and was often mistaken for being younger than his thirty-two years.

A few inches shorter than Ace, he was also leaner, giving him the kind of build better suited for competing in rodeos, which he did at every opportunity. There wasn't a championship buckle he didn't covet, an event at which he didn't excel. And yet, he never seemed satisfied.

There had been a time when Ace was the better bareback bronc rider, and he still participated once in a while for fun or to blow off steam. As long as it didn't interfere with work.

Another glaring difference between him and his brother. Ace put the ranch and family first. Colt, himself. He got away with doing less because, in Ace's opinion, their mother let him.

In truth, so did Ace. Love and loyalty were nothing if not complicated.

What infuriated him the most was Ace knew Colt to be capable of so much more. His brother had true skill with horses and cattle, too. The kind of skill Ace envied. If Colt would just take life and himself a little more seriously, he'd astound everyone with his accomplishments.

And, possibly, Ace could relinquish some of his responsibilities around the ranch. Particularly in light of the fact he was going to be a father.

"Thought I should let you know I'm leaving Thursday for the Crazy Eights Rodeo."

"Any chance you skip this one? We're examining the mares on Thursday. Prepping them for breeding season next month."

"Sorry, bro. I'm behind in steer wrestling and bull riding. I can't afford to miss one weekend if I expect to qualify for Nationals."

"December's a long way away."

"Every rodeo counts."

Ace was wasting his time, but he couldn't stop himself. "I need your help. Darrell's girls are on school break. He's taking the week off."

"I can do it Monday."

"That's my surgery day."

"Then Tuesday."

"Forget it." Ace didn't bother reciting his list for Tuesday. Nothing short of a catastrophe would stop Colt from going to the rodeo in Bozeman. "I'll just work Sunday."

Another day of rest spent toiling. Ace should be used to it by now. Instead, he was tired and cranky.

"I'll help you with the stock for the Western Frontier Pro Rodeo," Colt offered.

He'd help because he was competing in that one, too.

"I realize you've got a lot on your plate right now," Colt continued, "what with the new breeding business and all."

"Do you?"

"Sure."

Ace sensed his brother's guard rise like an invisible shield in front of him.

"Then why can't you stay home this one weekend?"

"I told you. I'm behind in two events."

"Is making all-around cowboy more important to you than this ranch?"

"Hey, I respect you and what you do. You could return the favor."

"What I do is work. Damn hard. I don't gallivant around the countryside, chasing dreams."

"You chase dreams." Colt's gaze traveled to Midnight. "They're just here."

"This family needs you, Colt."

"This family has you."

"And if they didn't?"

Colt grinned. "Not going to happen."

"It might. Things change."

"Yeah, like what? We strike oil?"

"I have my own family."

Colt laughed. "You need a woman for that, or hasn't anyone told you?"

"Flynn's pregnant. I'm the father."

"I…" Colt took a step back, caught his breath. "I had no idea you and she were dating."

"We're not."

"Then how—"

"Long story."

"You're smiling."

Ace had been doing that a lot since yesterday. "I'm excited about the baby."

"You are?"

"Hell, yes. Why wouldn't I be?"

"I don't know. Are you ready to be a dad?"

"I'll be ready by the time the baby's born. I like kids. I've always wanted to have my own."

It was another area he and Colt seemed to differ. Ace's brother had never expressed any interest in settling down, much less starting a family.

"Then I'm glad for you." Colt's flat voice sounded anything but glad.

"What's wrong?"

"How did Mom take the news?"

"I haven't told her yet. I will at dinner."

"Good luck with that."

"You think she won't be happy?"

"She and Dad always wanted us to be married before we had kids."

"Yeah, well, I'm not." He would be, if Flynn weren't so stubborn.

"I need to hit the road."

"Colt. Hey, come on, man. Stay. I'm going

to be spending a lot of time with Flynn while we figure things out. I could really use you."

"Maybe if I win this weekend, some of the pressure will be off."

The pressure his brother was under didn't compare to Ace's. He could feel it building inside him, a band stretched tight on the verge of snapping. But he maintained his cool, willed himself to calm down. Colt wouldn't change, and Ace refused to be like their late father, whose favorite method of motivating his children had been to verbally berate them.

Or had Ace, as the oldest, been pushed harder than his siblings?

"Fine," he said tightly. "Remember to call Mom, let her know you arrived. She worries."

"Yeah. And congratulations again. Flynn's a terrific gal."

Colt left, his gait just shy of a dead run.

Ace remained at the fence, watching him. His brother was always in a hurry to leave the ranch behind, but this exit was particularly hasty.

Strange.

Hopefully when Ace told the rest of his family about Flynn and the baby, they'd react better.

Ace resumed his chore of cleaning the saddle, his concentration a shambles. He'd pretty much decided to quit for the day and tackle Midnight's behavior problems tomorrow, when he felt something behind him. Startled, he patted his back pockets.

Son of a gun!

He spun slowly around.

Midnight stood a few feet away, smugly crunching a carrot.

Ace grabbed another one and held it out to the horse.

He snorted and retreated a step, still chewing.

"That's okay," Ace said, his anger at his brother dissipating. "It's a start."

A *very good* start.

The stock pens at the Western Frontier Pro Rodeo were already half-full when Ace and Colt arrived and parked their truck and trailer. Behind them were two more Thunder Ranch rigs, one carrying bucking horses and the other a pair of their most promising bulls.

Beau and Duke, Ace's twin cousins, had come along to help with the livestock and compete with Colt and Ace. It had been over a year since all four of them went up against each other at the same rodeo. Ace was looking forward to it.

His decision to enter bareback bronc riding was likely the only reason he and his brother hadn't argued since Colt's return from Bozeman last week. Ace had entered today not to mend their differences but to show up his brother. Beating Colt would feel good. It would also prove Ace still remembered how to have fun and wasn't, as his mother liked to call him, a stick in the mud.

She'd taken the news of Flynn's pregnancy well. More than well, she'd been thrilled. True to Colt's prediction, she expressed her desire to see Ace and Flynn married first, a natural reaction for most parents in Ace's opinion. But she'd been happy for Ace. So had Dinah, who'd rushed over after getting off duty to celebrate with them. The only damper to the evening had been Colt. Rather than join them, he'd found some reason to retreat to his room.

Ace, his cousins and the ranch crew had barely started unloading the livestock when Colt made a beeline away from the stock pens.

"Hey, where you going?" Ace hollered after him.

"The entry booth, to sign in."

"It can wait. The rodeo doesn't start for four more hours."

"I won't be long." Colt, jogging backward, raised his hand in a farewell gesture.

Ace took his frustration out on the toolbox mounted to the side of the trailer and the finicky padlock securing the lid.

"Beau and Duke have left to sign in, too." Harlan came up beside Ace. "You should go."

Ace spared the ranch hand a brief glance, then returned to searching for the pliers he swore were right on top when he'd last checked the toolbox. "There's still time."

"Royce and I can finish here and then transport the stock for tonight's events."

"I don't want to leave you two with all the work." Moving ornery bulls and horses was a lot to handle, even for two of the Harts' most experienced hands.

"Why not?" Harlan plucked the pliers out from under a socket set and held them out to Ace. "That's our job, what you pay us for."

The idea did appeal to him, and he could sure enough use a break.

It had been a tough week. Not a day went by he didn't put in ten or twelve hours, then fall into bed shortly after supper, exhausted. Making matters worse, Flynn had given him every excuse in the book not to see him. Yeah, they'd talked on the phone, but she refused to reconsider her plans of moving to Billings. Every call had ended on a terse note.

Ace wasn't having any better luck with Midnight. Other than persuading the horse to accept a few more treats, he'd made no real progress.

"Go on," Harlan encouraged. "This might be your last chance to compete for a while."

True. With the baby coming, Ace planned on spending most weekends at home, hopefully with Flynn. He didn't let himself think about spending his weekends driving back and forth to Billings to visit his child.

He slammed shut the lid to the toolbox, the knot of tension between his shoulders throbbing. The long hours and constant demands were having an effect on him. Eight bone-crunching seconds on the back of a wildly bucking bronc might be just the ticket to alleviate his stress.

"I won't be long." Ace repeated his brother's words to Harlan, the irony not lost on him.

"Bring some cold drinks back with you. Royce and I are parched."

Ace cut across the lot, which was reasonably dry thanks to several days of fair weather. The nights were still chilly, however, and the bucking stock would be feeling frisky.

It was going to be a good rodeo.

Colt had already signed in and left the entry booth by the time Ace got there. He spotted his brother near the arena entrance, talking to an attractive barrel racer.

Figures.

"I reckon they'll let just about anybody enter," a familiar voice behind Ace said.

He turned and grabbed the outstretched hand of his buddy Austin Wright, shaking it briskly. "I guess I'm going to have some competition today."

"Looks like it." Austin's affable grin was the same one Ace remembered from when they were young.

"What are you doing here?" he asked. "Thought you were chained to that tack shop of yours."

"I break loose once in a while."

Ace and Austin had grown up together, attended the same schools, the same church and vied for the attention of the same girls. They'd been fierce competitors on the basketball court as well as in the rodeo arena and good friends the rest of the time. In the years since high school they'd grown apart, despite living in the same town. In part because of Ace's grueling schedule, in part because of Austin's family situation. A father serving time for cattle rustling in a ranching community was a lot to live down.

"Let's get together later tonight," Ace said.

"I'd like that. After I embarrass you in the arena."

"Feeling lucky today?"

"Against you? Always."

"Loser buys dinner?"

"You're on." They shook hands again to seal their bet. "I heard you expanded your string."

"We did." Ace moved forward in line. "Brought a few of the new head with us today. They're coming on strong."

"Wish I'd drawn one."

"I pulled a McKinley bronc."

"Isn't he selling off?"

"He has some contracts still to fulfill over the next couple months." Ace found himself grinning, like he did every time he thought of Flynn and the baby. "There's something else. I'm going to be a dad."

"No fooling!"

Ace summarized the story of him and Flynn, omitting the details of their one-night stand.

"That's great." Austin beamed. "I'm really happy for you."

Why couldn't Colt be happy for Ace, too?

He and Austin continued chatting until it was Ace's turn to sign in. After Austin finished and they said their goodbyes, Ace made a quick stop at the concession stand before heading back to the livestock pens. Just as he walked up, two McKinley rigs rumbled on by—Earl behind the wheel of the first truck, Flynn beside him in the passenger seat.

Flynn!

She hadn't mentioned coming this weekend.

He checked in with Harlan and delivered the cold drinks, all the while keeping an eye on the truck with Flynn. When it came to a stop, the side door opened and she scrambled out. She then jogged around to the rear of the trailer and began directing her father as he backed up to a row of empty pens.

Ace hastened over and waited until Earl was finished parking before addressing Flynn.

"Hey, what are you doing here?"

"Same as you. Bringing stock."

Ace was prepared to toss her over his shoulder and carry her off if she attempted to help unload the horses. Fortunately she didn't, leaving the task to her dad and his trio of ranch hands.

Ace hadn't seen Flynn's father since the auction and braced himself for a stern talking-to. It's what he'd do in the other man's shoes.

"Afternoon, Earl," he said with a nod, and waited.

Earl went about his business, ignoring Ace.

He glanced at Flynn.

She shrugged.

"Sir, about the baby—"

Earl straightened, walked calmly over to Ace and stuck a finger in his chest. "I like you. But if you hurt my little girl, mark my word, there will be hell to pay."

"I won't hurt her, I swear."

"Glad that's settled."

"Me, too."

Earl poked Ace in the chest again before leaving.

Flynn laughed under her breath.

Ace wasn't amused and wiped a hand

across his damp brow. "Is that a good idea, you being here? What with the baby and all?"

"What do you mean?"

"Bucking stock aren't known for their manners."

"I'm not going to ride the horses." She laughed again.

Though, in Ace's opinion, the situation was serious, her gaiety was a welcome change from their recent strain.

"Just being near them is risky. They kick. Bite. Charge."

"I promise to be supercautious if you promise to be less obsessive."

"I care about you, Flynn." Much more than she realized.

Instead of becoming prickly, she smiled softly. "Thank you."

Grateful for whatever had caused the change in her, Ace let the cozy sensation her smile triggered wind through him.

If only it could be like this between them every day.

"Speaking of taking risks." She pointed to the entrant number he carried in his hand. "I should scold you for the same thing. What if you get hurt?"

"I'll withdraw," he said immediately.

"No." She laughed again. "I don't want you to change just because we're having a baby."

We? He liked her referring to them as a couple.

"Our child is more important to me than bronc riding."

"Rodeoing's a big part of your life. It's your business."

"But not competing. I won't be any good to either of you if I'm injured and unable to make a living. This gives me the excuse I need to quit without embarrassing myself."

"Compete, Ace. You like it and, be honest, you miss it."

"Sometimes." He'd been at the peak of his rodeo career back in college when they'd dated. He gave it up after his father died, like he had Flynn.

What if he'd been wrong all those years ago on both counts?

Their attention was drawn to the McKinley horses, who fussed and squealed and nipped at each other as they settled into the pen.

Flynn knitted her brows as she scrutinized them. "Hmm."

"Something wrong?"

"It's Fancy Gal." She started toward the fence. Ace followed her, determined to intervene if a horse so much as looked sideways at her. "She's been acting out of sorts all morning."

"Which one is she?"

Flynn pointed to a stout dun mare standing at the far end of the pen. Ears pinned back, teeth bared and swinging her head from side to side, she sent an unmistakable warning to her pen mates: stay away.

"She's one of my favorites and is usually pretty docile outside the arena."

"Want me to examine her?"

Relief lit Flynn's features. "Would you? I don't want to be a bother. You have your own string to worry about."

"I don't mind."

"I'll get her."

"You're not going in that pen with all those horses." Ace put a hand on her arm. "Your dad can do it."

She sighed. "All right."

Ace liked her when she was agreeable.

He was rather confident it wouldn't last.

Chapter 6

Pregnancy suited Flynn. She'd woken up that morning on completely the *right* side of the bed. Not that her doubts about the future had vanished. Far from it. But she felt good. Happy. Optimistic.

Her exuberance, however, dimmed as her concern for Fancy Gal escalated. The mare was clearly distressed and in pain.

It didn't take long for her father to separate the mare from the rest of the string, bring her out and tie her to the side of the trailer.

Flynn hovered near Ace as he conducted his examination. She had her suspicions about what ailed the mare and was curious to see if she was right.

"We probably shouldn't have brought her today." She stroked Fancy Gal's nose. Away from her pen mates, the mare was gentle as a lamb and calmly tolerated Ace's poking and prodding. "She's nineteen. Too old for competing."

"Not really," he said. "If they're in good health, horses can be competed into their twenties. But if you want to retire her, she'd make a nice broodmare."

"I hope whoever buys her does exactly that."

Ace ran a hand along Fancy Gal's abdomen. "Besides irritability, what are her other symptoms?"

Flynn pointed to the mare's shuffling hooves. "She keeps shifting her weight."

"I checked her feet," her father added, coming over. "No stones or abscesses or any problems that I saw."

"You won't take offense if I also have a look?" Ace picked up the mare's front hoof, braced it between his knees and dug around the soft underside with a penknife.

"I'd think you were a sorry vet if you didn't." Her father carefully supervised Ace's every move. Fancy Gal was one of his favorite horses, too.

Ace repeated the process with the remaining hooves. "They look fine." He took a step back and considered the mare. "Any signs of colic?"

"Nope."

"Yes," Flynn interjected. Colic was her guess. "She's been biting her flanks."

Ace placed his ear against Fancy Gal's abdomen.

Flynn held the mare's head firmly in place. Fancy Gal might be a lamb but sick animals often spooked and behaved out of character.

Ace straightened, his mouth set in a firm line. "Sounds like a war zone in there. I don't think you should compete her today."

"Poor girl," Flynn cooed, and scratched Fancy Gal behind the ears.

"Have we caught it in time?" her father asked.

He had reason to be concerned. Several years ago they had almost lost a prize gelding to a sudden and aggressive case of colic.

"I think so," Ace said. "Can you arrange for a separate stall or pen? She shouldn't be with the other horses."

"I'll talk to the barn manager."

"I can walk her," Flynn offered when her father left.

When their gelding had colic, she and her father had taken turns walking him all through the night. It had probably saved the gelding's life.

Ace shook his head. "I'd feel better if you got one of the men to do it."

"Fancy Gal won't hurt me."

"Not intentionally."

"I appreciate your concern, but I'm going to walk her and—"

"And I'm not stopping you," he finished for her.

"Something like that." Flynn squared her shoulders.

Ace's glance traveled from Fancy Gal to Flynn. "I don't like it."

"You have to trust me."

He groaned as if giving in to her caused him pain. "I've got some bute paste in my truck. That should help her with the discomfort." He promptly returned, a tube clutched in his hand, and administered the bute paste.

Fancy Gal didn't like the taste or the texture. She worked her jaw and rolled her tongue until the medication had dissolved.

Afterward, Ace accompanied Flynn and

Fancy Gal to the vacant pasture on the far side of the warm-up arena. She started to tell him to leave, that she was fine on her own, then reconsidered. She liked him walking beside her. She reconsidered again the third time his arm brushed hers.

At the end of their first circuit, Flynn told Ace, "You should probably go. Your event is the first one after the opening ceremony."

"If she worsens or shows any other symptoms, call me immediately. I don't care what I'm doing."

"We'll be fine."

He acted as if he hadn't heard her. "I'll stop by in an hour to check on her."

"You don't have to do that."

"Yes, I do. You were lucky today. She's in the early stages of colic. A few more hours, her chances of making a full recovery would be a lot less."

Whatever personal issues she had with Ace, she couldn't deny he was a good vet.

"I know it's a lot to ask, and you just acquired all those horses at the auction..."

"Tell me."

"Dad's selling all the livestock. I want Fancy Gal to go to a good home, one where she can live out the rest of her life." Flynn fiddled with the mare's lead rope. "She's really almost never sick. And she would make a wonderful broodmare. I can get you a copy of her registration papers—"

"You want me to buy her?"

"Yes."

When he didn't answer right away, Flynn's heart sank.

"It was a stupid idea."

"No, it isn't. I just don't like doing anything that will make your leaving easier."

She glanced away, hiding her disappointment.

He took her chin in his fingers and tilted her face to his. "But I'll buy her."

"Seriously? Because I don't want you doing this strictly for me."

"Of course I'm doing it for you. And she'd be a sound investment."

"Thank you, thank you!" Flynn threw herself at Ace and squeezed him tightly around the waist with her one free arm.

"Before you get carried away, we should probably talk price."

"I'll make sure Dad gives you a smoking deal."

Flynn sighed contentedly. This hug was so much nicer than the stiff one they'd shared at the fishing hole when she'd told him about the baby.

"In that case, maybe we should buy more of your father's horses."

"Oh, Ace." She stood on her tiptoes and impulsively pressed her lips to his cheek. The familiar scent of him instantly assailed her, weakened her knees so that she was forced to lean on him.

He went still.

Uh-oh. Big mistake.

She was about to pull away when he bent his head and sought her lips.

The kiss, light, tender and achingly sweet, lasted only a few seconds before he abruptly withdrew.

Not again!

Why was he always doing this to her?

Flynn stepped away, only to spy her father at the edge of the pasture, his gaze riveted on her and Ace.

Flynn gave Fancy Gal one last thorough inspection before permitting herself to relax. The mare was better, nosing around the corners of her pen for a tidbit of hay rather than exhibiting signs of distress.

True to his word, Ace had stopped by earlier and examined her, noting her progress and advising Flynn to continue walking the mare at intervals for the rest of the afternoon, possibly into the evening. He also brought some warm bran mash to settle Fancy Gal's stomach, though where he acquired it Flynn had no clue.

"I have my connections," was all he'd admit before returning to the arena.

She glanced at her watch, straining to hear the announcements coming from the direction of the arena. Ace's event, bareback bronc riding, would be starting soon. She was just locking up the truck when her father strode over. He hadn't mentioned seeing her and Ace kissing earlier, but she wouldn't put it past him.

What a mistake! Why did she continually lose her head with Ace?

Unfortunately, there was no going back now.

"Did I tell you Ace drew True Grit?" her father asked.

"Seriously? No, you didn't."

The gelding was one of her father's best bucking broncs—or worst, if you were the cowboy trying to ride him.

When her father began reciting the other bronc/cowboy matchups, Flynn cut him off.

"Ace hasn't been in a rodeo since last fall. True Grit's a lot of horse, even for someone who competes regularly."

"That's how rodeo works. It's the luck of the draw."

Bad luck, Flynn thought. "What if he gets injured?"

"He's a big boy."

"He's also the father of my child. Your grandchild."

Her father chuckled.

Flynn took off at a brisk walk.

He chased after her. "Where you going?"

"To tell Ace not to compete."

"What with the way you're acting, a person might suspect you have more feelings for him than you're willing to admit."

"This has nothing to do with me or my feelings."

Her father's persistent chuckling grated on Flynn's nerves.

She seldom ventured behind the bucking chutes where the participants gathered to assess the horses and their competition and to while away the time while they waited—usually nervously—for their turn.

Ace was there, along with his brother, cousins and Austin Wright. The moment he saw her, he broke away and met her halfway.

"Is Fancy Gal all right?" he asked.

"She's great."

"Are *you* all right?"

"Ace, don't compete."

"What?"

"Dad told me you drew True Grit. You know his reputation and his ranking."

"I'll be fine."

"See," her dad said, catching up with Flynn. "I told you."

"Please, Ace."

A twinkle lit his eyes. It also warmed her heart.

She was such a sucker.

"Weren't you just saying I shouldn't change because we're having a baby?"

"Yes, but True Grit is—"

"It's okay." He reached out and stroked her cheek.

"Promise me." She closed her eyes and sighed softly.

"I tend to agree with my daughter," Earl said. "True Grit probably has more giddyup than you're used to."

"Dad!" Flynn's eyes flew open.

Ace let his hand drop and turned to appraise her father. "I might be a little rusty, but I'm pretty sure I can sit that horse for eight seconds."

"That boast has all the makings of a wager."

Now Flynn was really upset. "No betting!"

Ace grinned. "What do you have in mind?"

"Flynn mentioned you're interested in buying Fancy Gal and maybe a few more of my string. I've got another potential buyer lined up. Hoyt Cammeron."

"Yeah?" Ace visibly perked up.

"You last the full eight seconds on True Grit, and I'll sell you any of my string you want and throw in Fancy Gal for free. You eat dirt, I sell the string to Hoyt, including Fancy Gal if he wants her."

"You can't," Flynn objected.

"You're on." Ace stuck out his hand to her father.

"Ace, get over here," Colt hollered. "Beau's up next."

"See you at the stock pens when I'm done." Ace squeezed Flynn's arm, then nodded curtly at her father.

"I'll be there, too. With Hoyt," Flynn's father added.

She waited a mere second after Ace left

before whirling on her father. "How could you, Dad? A bet? Really? And what's this with Hoyt? You told me you'd no more sell that man a broken-down pony than any of your string."

There was that chuckle again.

She groaned with frustration.

"Come on." He placed a hand on the small of her back and guided her toward the stands. "We'd better hurry before it's Ace's turn."

At her wit's end, Flynn went with her father to the crowded bleachers where they found two empty seats. Second to the last row, unfortunately. She couldn't remain still as one cowboy after the other went. Beau did well, his score landing him in the lead. His position lasted only until Austin Wright's turn. Austin had also drawn a McKinley horse and was the first competitor that day to successfully ride one.

Finally, after what felt like forever, Ace's name was called.

Flynn gnawed her lower lip as she watched him straddle the fence and sit True Grit. The horse, raring to go, shifted nervously in the narrow chute, bumping into the side panels and tossing his head.

Ace didn't hurry.

He was too far away for Flynn to see, but she imagined him testing the rigging and adjusting his grip on the handle until it satisfied him. He'd place his feet above the horse's shoulders, correctly marking the horse before entering the arena so as not to be disqualified before his ride even started. He'd listen to the advice of his brother and cousins and buddies who were clustered together and hanging on the fence.

In the end, he'd trust his instincts.

Suddenly, the chute gate flew open and True Grit exploded into the arena, front hooves solidly planted on the ground, his back ones reaching for the sky. Not the biggest horse there by any means, his claim to fame was his ability to bend himself into the shape of a twist tie while achieving incredible heights.

Today was no exception.

Rocking onto his hind legs, True Grit reared, standing almost completely vertical. Ace clung to the rigging, leaning so far back his head lay against the horse's rump and the toes of his boots touched the horse's ears. Even in that impossible position, Ace spurred the horse, urging him to buck higher, buck harder.

True Grit gave it his all, hitting the ground with his front feet and spinning in a full circle with such force, Ace was almost knocked off.

Flynn gasped and covered her mouth with her hand.

What was wrong with the timer? Surely eight seconds had passed. More like a full minute.

True Grit executed another gravity-defying buck, his goal to fling Ace over his head and into the stands. By some miracle, Ace hung on.

The buzzer went off. Instantly, Flynn was out of her seat. "He did it!"

Applause and cheers broke out from the crowd as the pickup men surrounded Ace, hauled him off the horse and deposited him—still in one piece, thank God—onto the ground. As Ace walked across the arena, he picked up his hat from where it had fallen and waved it at the crowd.

Flynn started toward the aisle.

Her father grabbed her wrist, waylaying her. "Where are you going?"

To congratulate Ace, but she didn't want to tell her father that. "Walk Fancy Gal."

"Don't you want to see Ace's score?"

It didn't matter to her, only that he'd finished. "Sure." She sat back down.

A few seconds later, Ace's score was blasted from the speakers while simultaneously appearing on the scoreboard.

"Eighty-three," her father muttered. "Not great, not bad."

"Pretty good for someone who only competes occasionally."

"I'm glad to see him get Fancy Gal and whatever other horses he wants."

"Not Hoyt Cammeron?"

"Hoyt was never interested."

"What!" Flynn stood, braced her hands on her hips and glared at her father. "Then why the bet with Ace?"

"It was for you."

"Me?"

"I wanted to see how bad he wants you. How hard he's willing to fight."

"This was about the horses," she insisted.

"No, it wasn't. And he knows it, too."

"You're crazy."

"Maybe so." Her father wore a smug smile. "But now we have an answer."

Ace reached for his ringing cell phone, groaning in agony as every muscle in his body rebelled. Gracie's number appeared on the display. "Yeah," he barked.

"You said to call you when Flynn McKinley arrived."

"Thanks. Have her meet me at the main paddock." He disconnected, let his phone drop onto the mattress and didn't move for a full two minutes.

Finally, when he'd mustered enough strength, he pushed to a sitting position with the agility of a ninety-year-old man and lowered his feet to the floor.

Two days since the Western Frontier Pro Rodeo, and he still hurt like a son of a bitch.

Lasting eight seconds in bareback bronc riding and winning his bet with Earl had been great. Finishing in seventh place and beating out his brother and cousins, even better. He didn't even mind buying a steak dinner for his friend Austin, who'd finished second.

Thank goodness Ace hadn't qualified for the finals on Sunday. He'd be a cripple. Colt, Beau and Duke had been left with overseeing the loading of the livestock for the long, *long* return trip home during which Ace had suffered their endless ribbing. Deserved ribbing. What had made him think he could compete once or twice a year and not come away feeling as though he'd gone for a joyride inside a cement mixer?

Rising from the bed, he tucked his shirt into his pants, put on his boots and grabbed his hat off his dresser. Break time was officially over.

He hobbled through the adjacent sitting area and out a door that lead to an enclosed patio. Some years ago, when it became apparent Ace would be staying on the ranch and helping his mother, he'd remodeled two of the downstairs bedrooms into a master suite with a private outside entrance. That way he could come and go at all hours, one of the hazards of being a vet, without disturbing the rest of the household.

Plus, Ace liked his solitude—until lately, anyway.

Waking up next to Flynn had been nice, her smooth, warm curves snuggled next to him, her hand folded inside his even in sleep.

Then he'd realized what a mistake he'd made. Not sleeping with her, but letting her get close. Letting her glimpse the raw need he ruthlessly kept concealed behind a competent, take-charge exterior.

Ace wasn't weak like his father had been.

He wouldn't use alcohol or berate others to compensate for his insecurities.

His Polaris sat parked beside the patio entrance in its usual spot. The all-terrain vehicle was his usual mode of transportation around the ranch when not riding a horse.

There would be no riding horses for several more days if the ibuprofen he'd been swallowing like Halloween candy didn't kick in soon.

Starting the Polaris, he drove to the paddock, the same paddock where they'd put Wally Dunlap's mares after the auction. The drive took only a few minutes. A bumpy, excruciating, teeth-grinding few minutes.

He expected to find Earl or one of the McKinley hands with Flynn, only she'd come by herself.

"Thanks, Gracie," he told the ranch hand after crawling out of the Polaris.

She picked up on his cue. Striding toward the barn, she said, "See ya later, Flynn."

"Geez, Ace, are you all right?" Flynn gave him a concerned once-over, taking in his bent posture.

"It's nothing."

She covered her mouth and laughed.

"Not funny." He went to the back of the

horse trailer and inspected the five mares and one gelding inside, Fancy Gal and True Grit among them.

"It is too funny." She came up behind him, trying not to smirk. "That'll teach you to bust broncs without getting into condition first."

It would. If he were smart, he'd quit rodeoing for good. He couldn't afford to be laid up.

Unless he and Flynn had a son. Then he'd teach their boy everything about horses and cattle and ranching and rodeoing. On second thought, he'd teach the same things to a daughter.

A fresh wave of determination surged inside him. There would be a new generation of Harts. Rebuilding their flagging business, securing the future, took on a whole new meaning. As did carrying on family traditions, instilling in his children a love and respect for the land and the animals that inhabited it.

Wait a minute. Children?

Who exactly was he planning on having more children with? Flynn had turned down his marriage proposal. She was also moving to Billings.

He unlatched the rear door on the trailer, suppressing a groan.

"Wait, I'll help." Flynn reached for the handle and instantly withdrew when their hands touched. "You, um, don't want to injure yourself any worse than you already have."

There'd been a time when she wouldn't have been jumpy around him.

Was that a good sign?

"Cut me some slack," he joked in an attempt to relieve the awkwardness. "I'm getting enough grief from everyone else as it is."

He opened the trailer door, wincing at the pain. Maybe he should have accepted her help.

Eventually, all six horses were unloaded and exploring the paddock. Ace and Flynn stood side by side at the fence, watching them.

"You picked the best from my dad's string," she observed.

"Yeah." Ace was pretty happy about his selection. Several of the horses were nothing special to look at, but they could buck, and that was what counted. "Fancy Gal have any more problems with colic?"

"None, and I've kept a close eye on her."

"How are *you* feeling?"

"Good. Fantastic, in fact."

"No nausea?"

"A little last night."

"When's your next doctor appointment?"

"May first."

"I'll go with you."

Flynn pushed off the fence. "There's no need."

"I want to."

She started back toward the truck.

Ace caught up with her, though it was with some difficulty. "What's the matter? You don't want me to go?"

"It's not that." She shoved her hands into her down vest pockets. "What's going to happen when I leave?"

"With your doctor appointments?"

She sighed. "The more attached you get, the harder it will be."

"I'm going to be attached to my kid."

"I was talking about me."

"We agreed we're going to try and get along. Do things together."

"Getting along doesn't include kissing."

She had him there. "Was it so awful?" he asked, attempting a wry grin. "You did participate."

Her defenses visibly shot up. "You're missing the point."

"I don't think I am." He waited until she'd

shut the trailer door. "Don't go to Billings, Flynn. Marry me."

"I told you no, and I told you why. Nothing's changed."

"You have to admit, there were some pretty serious sparks between us."

"Sparks aren't enough." She gazed at him pointedly. "Sometimes, love isn't enough. But it has to be there for a marriage to survive."

"Then don't marry me, but stay in Roundup. We need more time to figure this out."

Her expression fell, telegraphing her disappointment with his answer.

He scrambled to gain ground. "Our kid deserves to have both his parents raising him."

"Couples who live apart successfully raise children all the time. My parents did. Well, my dad did."

"And he ran a demanding business."

"But he always put me and my sister first. There wasn't a single dinner he missed." Her gaze fastened on him. "Can you make the same promise? Because I won't consider staying otherwise."

"I'm willing to change."

"How?"

"Once the business is operating profitably

and the loan is paid down, I'll cut back on my hours."

"When will that be?"

"A year. Possibly a little longer." In reality, it would be more like three years.

"You haven't cut back in the last ten years," she said skeptically.

"Yeah, but now there's a baby on the way."

"Which is all the more reason for you to focus on your family's business. It's your livelihood. I can't support this baby on my own."

And he'd promised to take care of his child. He couldn't do that with only the income from his vet practice. Neither could he saddle his mother with the entire responsibility of managing the ranch and paying down the loan.

His determination returned tenfold. He'd do it all, work and be there for Flynn. Be a better man than his father.

"Give me a chance to prove myself."

"I am. That's what we're doing."

"If we were married, there—"

"I was married to Paul, and it didn't make a bit of difference. He still put his career above me." She headed for the cab of her truck. "There's no reason for me to think you'll be any different."

"I'm going to continue proposing until you say yes."

"That should be interesting," she said over her shoulder, "since I'm going to continue saying no until you propose for the right reasons."

"What's more important than our child?"

"You should be asking yourself, what's *just as* important as our child."

Chapter 7

Flynn stepped into the stark, utilitarian lobby of the Roundup Sheriff Station, a white plastic grocery bag clenched in her hand. She came here on occasion to visit Dinah and once when she was a senior in high school. Dinah, Flynn and a few of their friends had been questioned in the matter of a teenage prank that had involved drinking and several cans of spray paint.

Flynn had been innocent. Dinah, a little less innocent. Funny, her friend was now the sheriff and the one questioning delinquent teenagers.

A lot had changed since those days. Flynn

would have never guessed she'd be married and divorced, living at home again and about to embark on single motherhood.

"Is Sheriff Hart in?" she asked the male deputy behind the counter.

"Your name?"

"Flynn McKinley."

She took a seat on a bench in the lobby to wait. Dinah appeared a few minutes later, a bright smile on her face, her khaki uniform neatly pressed.

Seeing her friend often gave Flynn a start. Dinah closely resembled Ace, though her eyes were hazel as opposed to brown. Even so, there was no mistaking their relation.

"Hey, what are you doing here?"

"I brought you a peace offering." Flynn held out the plastic bag.

Dinah peeked inside at the package of miniature Snickers bars and grinned wickedly. "Come on back." She led Flynn down the hall and to her office. "Not sure why you think you need to bring me a peace offering, but I won't complain."

Snickers bars were one of Dinah's guilty pleasures.

Behind the privacy of her closed door, Dinah gave Flynn the brief hug she wouldn't in front of the other deputies and clerical staff.

"What's up?"

"I wanted to apologize."

"Did you do anything requiring an apology?" Dinah sat behind her desk while Flynn settled in the chair across from her.

The package of candy was opened, and a handful of bars quickly distributed between them. The image of Dinah, all proper and official in her uniform and chomping on candy, brought a smile to Flynn's face.

"I should have told you about the baby," she said between bites. "Not waited until Ace did."

"No worries. I get it."

"I wasn't sure what I was going to do. Heck, I'm still not sure."

"Marry him," Dinah said matter-of-factly, catching Flynn off guard.

"Did Ace tell you he'd proposed?"

"He didn't have to. I know my brother." Dinah evaluated another Snickers bar before popping it in her mouth with a contented sigh. "When's the big day?"

And here Flynn had thought she'd be the one to break the news to her friend.

"There is no big day. I refused."

"Why? You love him."

"But he doesn't love me."

"Nonsense."

"Dinah, he doesn't."

"Ace holds his cards close to his chest. He's always been that way. Got worse after Dad died. He's afraid of being hurt."

It was hard for Flynn to imagine Ace as being afraid of anything. Then again, she'd seen his vulnerable side the night they'd made love and she'd conceived.

"I'm not sure I want to be married to a man who won't or can't express his emotions."

"Isn't that better than a man who tells you he loves you and doesn't mean it?"

She was referring to Paul.

"Selfishly, I'm asking you to give him a chance." Dinah made a pleading face. "There isn't anyone else I want for a sister-in-law."

"Me, either." Flynn didn't think there was anyone she'd rather have for a husband than Ace, but only if he returned her feelings.

"I love Colt and Tuf. They're great guys in their own way. But the truth is, if I were in a jam, Ace would be the first one I'd call. He'd come through for me. He will for you, too."

"Is it wrong to want a man who will sweep me off my feet?"

"Are you so sure he won't?"

"I thought he might. Once. Then he left. Ducked out of my bedroom like he'd done something wrong."

"Thank you, Dad." Dinah snorted and sat back in her chair.

"What does your dad have to do with this?"

"He had two sets of rules. One for us, one for him. He always put these unrealistic expectations on my brothers, Ace in particular. I wouldn't be surprised if Ace woke up the next morning thinking he'd wronged you. The guilt probably ate him alive."

"He had nothing to be guilty about."

"Try telling him that."

"Great." Flynn slumped in her chair. "He not only doesn't love me, he proposed to me out of guilt in addition to duty. Be still my foolish heart."

"Come on, that's not true."

"It is, according to what you just told me."

"Flynn, don't move to Billings. Not yet. Give Ace a little more time, he won't disappoint you. Once he gets the breeding business off the ground and the problems with Midnight resolved, he'll be able to think clearly, realize how he feels about you."

"Falling in love with someone isn't a decision you make. It's either there or it isn't."

"No, but letting yourself embrace that love *is* a decision."

Flynn wanted to talk to Dinah longer about Ace, except her desk phone rang.

"I've got to go," she said after hanging up, her formerly pleasant expression now grim. "Domestic dispute. A bad one."

"Thanks for seeing me."

"I miss you." Dinah hugged her again before walking out the door. "Let's have a girls' night out soon."

"Sounds good."

Dinah took off the moment they reached the lobby, shouting orders to the deputy behind the counter before disappearing through another door.

Flynn found herself a little in awe of her friend. Was this the same girl who'd giggled with her over teen magazines when they were twelve? The same woman who'd rebelled at seventeen and raised all kinds of hell?

Maybe Dinah was right and Flynn should give Ace another chance. Each of the Hart children bore scars thanks to their father's actions.

Was Flynn any different? Her own mother's abandonment had damaged her every bit as much as John Hart's betrayal did Ace.

No wonder her and Ace's relationship was such a mess.

"Are you sure about this?" Ace's mother asked, trepidation lending an unevenness to her voice.

"I don't think we have a choice," he answered. "We need to know one way or the other if we can use him, and we need to know before breeding season is in full swing."

Yesterday, Midnight had been moved from the pens at Ace's clinic to his permanent location in the stud quarters. His spacious stall opened out into a paddock. From there, he could see horses grazing in the near pastures and cattle in the far ones.

Gracie had been assigned the task of exercising Midnight an hour or more every day in the round pen. For some reason, he tolerated her better than Ace or any of the other ranch hands, allowing her to lead him to the pen and put him through his paces.

It was a development Ace found interesting and relevant. More than ever, he was convinced Midnight had been treated poorly at the hands of the livestock foreman and, as a result, distrusted people. Men in particular. Rehabilitating the horse, if he was indeed capable of being rehabilitated, would require time and patience and careful strategy.

A woman handler might provide the key.

Ace preferred not to isolate Midnight from his brethren. Horses were normally social animals. But until he could be handled without worry, they were better off safe than sorry.

There was, however, one exception.

Midnight was being put to the test for the first time.

Ace and his mother waited in the breeding shed for Gracie to retrieve Midnight from his quarters, connected to the breeding shed by a corridor. Ace had designed the facility himself as well as developing the stringent guidelines for their breeding program. An established routine and contained environment were both essential components of that program.

"How's Flynn?" His mother asked the question daily.

"Working too hard."

"At the clinic?"

"And for her dad. I wish she'd take it easier."

"Flynn's always been a go-getter. Has she had any luck enrolling in nursing school?"

"Not that she's mentioned."

After their disagreement last week, Ace and Flynn were back to communicating mostly by phone. He didn't pressure her, but she could only put him off so long. Her next doctor's appointment was in less than two weeks, and he would be there with her.

"Do you think she and Earl would come to Sunday brunch if I invited them?"

"You can ask." Ace liked the suggestion. Refusing his mother would be much harder than refusing him.

"She still resisting your charms?"

"Hard to believe, I know."

"Not that it's my business, but has it occurred to you that marrying her might not be the best idea?"

"What? I thought you were gung ho about all us kids being married first."

"That would be best, ideally. But I'm concerned if you somehow convince Flynn to marry you, you'll wind up alienating her."

"I've already promised her I'd try and cut back on work."

"I'm not talking about work. I'm talking about love. Flynn is a romantic. She isn't interested in marrying because it makes sense or is the right thing to do."

Ace was still digesting what his mother

said when a loud banging came from the direction of Midnight's quarters.

"Everything okay?" Ace hollered.

"We're good." Gracie's confident reply carried down the corridor.

"Aidan," his mother said. "She needs help."

"Gracie knows what she's doing."

Like him, his mother was nervous.

He debated going to investigate, prepared to step in at the first sign of trouble. But he'd rather not agitate Midnight if at all possible. They had a lot riding on today's outcome.

After double-checking Miss Kitty's lead rope, he craned his head to peer down the corridor.

What was the holdup?

He absently patted the mare, a rangy bay that had once been part of Wally Dunlap's string. She flicked her ears, her only sign of anticipation. None of this was new to her, she'd already borne two foals by Midnight. She was also fully in heat and receptive.

All things considered, she made a perfect candidate.

It was Ace's hope Midnight would get the job done without a fuss and without caring who else was in the breeding area with him.

A clattering of hooves on the concrete

floor accompanied a high-pitched squeal. Midnight and Gracie promptly burst into the breeding shed, a whirlwind of raw energy.

"Easy now." She gripped the stud chain firmly in both hands, but the horse was clearly in the driver's seat.

The instant Midnight spied Miss Kitty, he dialed into her. Prancing, snorting, his nostrils flaring, he showed off for her.

She did what came naturally, what her instincts dictated, and raised her tail.

Midnight went into a frenzy.

"Whoa, boy!" Gracie tugged, barely hung on.

Ace didn't think, he reacted. "Mom, get back!" He pushed his mother aside, then grabbed the stud chain from Gracie's hands.

Midnight tossed his head and ripped the chain from Ace's grasp. He had only one thing on his mind: Miss Kitty.

"Watch out!" Ace motioned for Gracie to stay back. It was too dangerous intervening at this point. Better to let nature take its course and hope for the best.

It was over within a minute. Midnight abandoned Miss Kitty, his interest waned.

When Ace reached for the stud chain, the

horse did an about-face. Huffing, he raced back down the corridor to his quarters.

Gracie started after him.

"Leave him," Ace ordered, angry at himself more than the horse. "He can't go anywhere." He turned to his mother. "You all right?"

She stepped forward, several shades paler than normal. "Well, that didn't go as planned."

Ace went over to inspect Miss Kitty, unhappy with what he saw. She'd suffered minor lacerations on her back and flanks, the result of Midnight's steel shoes. Luckily for all of them, she was familiar with Midnight and the breeding process. A different mare, and the results could have been disastrous.

"I think maybe we should sell him." Ace's mother watched over his shoulder as he cleansed and treated Miss Kitty's wounds.

"You could be right."

Gracie looked ready to cry.

"None of this is your fault," he assured her.

She sniffed. "I'll go shut his stall door."

Ace packed up his medical case, silently berating himself. He'd rushed. Midnight wasn't ready.

"None of this is your fault, either." His mother patted his arm.

"Yeah? I'm the one who insisted on buying him."

"And I supported you."

Gracie returned, relief evident on her face. "How is he?"

"Sweet as a lamb. All in a day's work to him."

Ace wasn't fooled. The good horse act wouldn't last.

He untied Miss Kitty's lead rope and handed it to Gracie. "Take her to my clinic."

"Wait, Gracie, I'll walk with you," his mother said. "I have some contracts in my office to sign and ship." She glanced over her shoulder at Ace. "You coming?"

He shook his head. "I'll catch up with you later."

He traveled the connecting corridor to Midnight's stall, observing the horse for several long moments. Midnight observed Ace in return, the same intelligent look in his eyes Ace had witnessed that day at the auction.

"You're going to have to do better next time," he said, realizing he wasn't ready to sell the horse.

Midnight lowered his head to the stall floor and blew lustily, shooting a cloud of the dry bedding into the air.

Stallions were typically a handful, but they could be taught manners. Midnight needed to learn some, or relearn them in his case.

"What happened to you after Wally got sick?"

Midnight snorted and stared inquisitively at Ace, all traces of fight and flightiness gone.

Was being bred to Miss Kitty or something else responsible for the difference?

An idea came to Ace. He jumped into his Polaris and drove to his office at the clinic. There, he made a phone call to Wally Dunlap's son, glad to reach the man on his first attempt, and identified himself as the new owner of Midnight.

"Can you tell me something about him?" he asked.

"Like what?"

"His history. Any problems. His care and routine."

"I'll try. I wasn't very involved in Dad's business."

"Did your father pasture Midnight with other horses or in separate quarters?"

"Both, I think. He had a system. Might have had to do with the season. Sometimes Midnight was in the pasture with other horses, sometimes by himself."

"Were the horses mares?"

"Could have been. Though, honestly, I don't remember Midnight being all that aggressive with geldings or other stallions, unless there was a mare in heat. Even then, he was able to be restrained. Dad couldn't have competed him in rodeos otherwise."

What Wally's son said was true.

"About the livestock foreman you hired, did he keep to your dad's system?"

"No. He said he preferred to house studs away from the other horses."

Ace asked the man a number of additional questions before thanking him and disconnecting.

He found his mother in her office on the opposite side of the barn.

"You going to be home for dinner tonight?" She closed the ledger she'd been reading and shut off her computer. "I'm making chili and corn bread."

"That's an offer I can't refuse."

"It'll be ready in a couple hours. How's Miss Kitty?"

"No worse for the wear." He sat in her visitor chair. "I spoke to Wally Dunlap's son just now."

"You called him?"

"I wanted information. I'm thinking of putting Midnight in the pasture with a few mares."

She drew back in surprise. "Is that wise?"

"According to Wally's son, Midnight got along with other horses and was regularly put to pasture with them." Ace summarized his phone conversation. "I think it's worth a try."

"When are you going to test your theory?"

"This afternoon. He's as calm as I've ever seen him."

"And if he hurts the mares like he did Miss Kitty?"

"We'll have him on a twenty-four-hour watch."

"You can't stay up all night."

"Gracie, Harlan and Royce will help. We'll take turns."

His mother smiled. "I'm glad you're not giving up on him. Or yourself."

"I still believe Midnight's the right horse for us to build our breeding business."

"That kind of tenacity will win over Flynn."

"You think?"

Her smile widened. "I'm counting on it."

So was Ace.

* * *

"He's a brand-new horse!" Gracie grinned exuberantly.

"I wouldn't go that far." Ace downplayed his excitement, which exceeded Gracie's. He didn't want to get ahead of himself only to be disappointed.

They'd pastured Midnight with the mares nearly a full twenty-four hours ago and, so far, it was going well. *Really* well.

"You have to admit," Gracie insisted, "beauty soothes the savage beast."

"Midnight clearly likes the ladies."

He reminded Ace more of a besotted puppy than a beast, following the mares around and pleading for their attention. What had happened to the fiery stallion from yesterday?

Ace had carefully selected the six mares he'd put with Midnight. All but one were from Wally Dunlap's string. At the last minute, Ace decided to include Fancy Gal. She possessed a solid, dependable temperament he hoped would rub off on Midnight.

One of the mares gave Midnight a little warning kick.

"I bet she won't be so standoffish next week," Gracie observed.

Probably not. Mares' cycles often accelerated when they were in the vicinity of a stallion.

"We need to diligently monitor them," Ace said. "If Midnight shows the least sign of aggression, I want him moved straightaway."

"I'm betting that won't happen."

Ace tended to agree. Right now, Midnight looked ready to roll over and have his tummy scratched.

"You came up with a good idea, boss."

"I don't know about that. Pasture breeding works fine for our mares. Any potential clients will want their mares hand bred."

Or inseminated artificially, but Ace was determined to worry about one obstacle at a time. Today, that was modifying Midnight's behavior enough to ensure a decent crop of foals next spring. Breeding season in Montana lasted only until the end of June. They either saw immediate progress or made the difficult decision to sell Midnight while there was still time to acquire another stud.

A few of the more friendly mares meandered over to the fence for the homemade horse treats Ace had gotten from Angie Barrington's horse rescue. He and Gracie willingly obliged them.

"Have you decided which of the livestock to take to the Torrington Rodeo?"

"True Grit, definitely, and I'd like to try Razorback. He's showing a lot of potential."

For the next several minutes, Ace and Gracie talked shop.

"I'd better see how that mechanic's coming along," Gracie said. "He promised to have the tractor repaired before the evening feeding." She sped off in one of the ranch's numerous ATVs.

The horses, startled by the noise, galloped away, stopping just as abruptly at the fence to nibble on lush green grass. All except for Midnight. He'd set his sights on Fancy Gal, perhaps because she was new.

"You like 'em a little older, huh?" Ace chuckled to himself as the stallion put on a show, prancing in circles around the mare, giving her affectionate nuzzles and nips on the neck and rump.

She took it all in stride, mostly ignoring him—which only encouraged him to try harder.

"She's a tough one, boy. You might pick a different mare."

There was no accounting for love, and

Midnight had been hit hard. He continued courting Fancy Gal, to no avail.

Ace was about to leave when Fancy Gal suddenly displayed a change of heart. Nickering softly, she returned Midnight's nuzzles.

"Well, I'll be damned."

The old girl wasn't so tough after all.

When Ace finally left several minutes later, the two horses were standing side by side, head to tail, Midnight resting his chin on Fancy Gal's hindquarters while she grazed unconcerned.

"Maybe I am a genius." Pleased with himself, Ace climbed into the Polaris, feeling almost as good about Midnight as he did about the prospect of becoming a father.

His mood promptly dimmed. If only Flynn were as easy to sway as Fancy Gal.

He could use a little of Midnight's luck when it came to the fairer sex.

Luck or persistence? Midnight was one determined fellow, and it had paid off.

Ace parked the Polaris outside his clinic, pushed back his cowboy hat and scratched his head.

All kidding aside, he could be on to something. The more Ace thought about it, the more convinced he became. He'd been wrong to jump the gun and propose to Flynn. Twice. She was understandably cautious after her unhappy marriage and painful divorce.

She was also understandably cautious after the way Ace had treated her. Any woman in her right mind would be.

What he needed to do was take a page from Midnight's book and woo Flynn. Patiently and persistently. Practice that tenacity his mother had mentioned.

Removing his cell phone from his belt, he dialed Flynn's number. She answered on the fourth ring. Had she been considering not taking his call?

"Hey, it's Ace. Did I catch you at work?" He'd forgotten evenings were the best time to reach her.

"It's all right, I'm on break."

He noted the hint of reservation in her voice but didn't let it deter him.

"I was wondering, are you free tomorrow evening?"

"What's up?"

"Pizza and wings at the Brick Oven." The restaurant was one of her favorites. "Unless you'd like to eat somewhere else?" A long pause followed. "Flynn? You still there?"

"Are you asking me on a date?"

"I am."

"Is there something you want to discuss?"

"No, I just want to take you out to eat."

"We're not, um, romantically involved."

They could be, if she gave them a chance.

"It's dinner. Between two people who happen to be having a baby and working toward establishing a healthy, solid relationship."

"I don't know…"

"Come on. You have to admit, things have been tense between us lately. Enjoying a casual meal on neutral territory will do us good."

Another longer pause followed. "O…kay."

Ace was glad she couldn't see the huge smile he wore. "What time are you off work?"

"Six."

"Is seven too early?"

"Seven's fine. But we can't have pizza. Spicy food doesn't sit well with me these days."

"Where'd you like to go?"

"It's beef Stroganoff night at the Number 1 Diner."

The place where it all started. Interesting that she would choose it.

"Great. And I promise, nothing but food's on the menu."

No kissing, no sneaking into her bedroom, no incredible, mind-bending sex.

"I'm going to hold you to that," she warned. "See you tomorrow."

He disconnected, his good mood restored. He had a dinner date with Flynn, and Midnight was settling in with his harem of mares.

Ace's day couldn't get any better.

Chapter 8

The smell of impending rain struck Flynn the moment she stepped from Ace's truck. She'd remembered a coat but forgotten an umbrella. Getting wet, however, was the least of her worries.

She and Ace were having dinner.

Not that they hadn't eaten together before—when they'd dated, of course, and on occasions when she'd joined the Harts for birthdays and holidays.

Then there had been the night of their indiscretion. Hard to believe that was almost two months ago.

"It's crowded," Ace commented as they

strolled across the parking lot to the diner's front entrance.

"The beef Stroganoff special is always popular."

The potpie special was also popular, which is what the restaurant had been serving the night Ace went home with her.

How in the world had that even happened?

She'd been on a date. Correction, was supposed to have been on a date. The guy had called at the last second, after she'd arrived at the diner to meet him, and canceled. Something about his clothes dryer malfunctioning. Seriously? She'd tried to convince herself she didn't care. He wasn't anyone important, she'd only agreed to go out with him because a mutual friend had set them up.

Rather than leave, Flynn had stayed and ordered dinner. To spite him, she supposed, and because she was hungry.

Ace had dropped by the diner on his way home from treating a yearling filly with a severe respiratory infection.

"Two tonight?" The hostess's question startled Flynn, returning her to the present. "Follow me." The woman grabbed two menus and escorted Flynn and Ace to a table that couldn't possibly be any more out in the open.

She cringed inside as Ace pulled out her chair. Discreetly scanning the room, she counted three familiar faces, nodding in response to their smiles of recognition. It could be worse. At least none of the Hart ranch hands were there.

Why had she suggested this place? She'd have been better off with pizza and wings and a case of heartburn.

She fingered the edge of the menu as she studied it, which was ridiculous since she knew the offerings by heart.

"Evening, folks." Their waitress, all of eighteen and cute as a button, flashed them a dimpled smile. "Can I get you something to drink?"

Ace waited for Flynn to order first.

"Umm…" Iced tea was out of the question, unfortunately. "Lemonade," she said with a sigh.

"Same for me."

"I thought you didn't like lemonade that much."

"Neither do you."

"I'd have iced tea if caffeine wasn't bad for the baby. No reason you can't."

"Lemonade's fine."

He was being sweet again, like at Thunder Creek when he'd proposed. She'd tell him that, except the last time hadn't gone well.

He'd also been sweet two months ago when he'd spotted her sitting alone at a table not far from this one, come over and asked her what was wrong. Funny, Flynn thought she'd been doing an admirable job hiding her disappointment about being stood up. But Ace had always been good at reading people, her more than most.

He'd sat and told her the other guy's loss was his gain, bought her dinner and regaled her with amusing stories of their errant childhood. By dinner's end, Flynn was having so much fun she couldn't even remember the guy's name.

Later, outside, she and Ace had kissed. Spontaneously. Lightly, at first. Then, in the span of a single softly issued moan, everything changed.

She was the one who'd suggested they go to her place. Her father was having a night out with his cronies and wouldn't be home until late. Ace had followed her in his truck. Flynn was convinced during the fifteen-minute drive that one or both of them would come to their senses. It didn't happen.

If anything, the clandestine nature of their

rendezvous added to the excitement. He'd parked his truck behind the barn, then met her at the kitchen door.

They couldn't stumble down the hall to her bedroom fast enough.

"How's work going?" Ace's voice penetrated Flynn's thoughts.

She blinked and set her menu down, acutely aware of the flush creeping up her neck and cheeks. She had to stop dwelling on that night. His touch. The tangled sheets strewn across his naked body.

"Fine. We've been busy this week. The flu seems to be going around."

"You need to be careful you don't get sick."

"I'll be okay. I don't have too much patient contact."

"As much as I hate the idea of you moving, I'd almost rather you were going to school than exposed to sick people all day."

"There are probably just as many sick people on campus."

"Sorry if I'm coming on too strong."

"You're…not."

Turning away from his charmingly crooked smile was a lot harder tonight than it had been at Thunder Creek. There, the dim restaurant lighting wasn't softening his features, reminding her of the younger Ace she'd fallen head over heels for.

They managed to make pleasant small talk for the remainder of the meal. Ace didn't bring up the baby again, her moving to Billings or school. The closest he came was when he asked, "Has your dad had any offers on the ranch?"

"No, and he's disappointed. A few people have come by, but they were more curious than anything else. The real estate agent keeps telling Dad it's a difficult market these days."

"I think more people are trying to sell their ranches than buy one."

"Or they're looking for a bargain. Dad's pretty set on his price."

"Did my mom call him about Sunday brunch at the house?"

"She did. I think it's set for next weekend."

The waitress appeared and removed their plates. "Can I interest you two in dessert? We have fresh-baked red velvet cake and key lime pie."

"No, thanks. But don't let me stop you," Flynn added when Ace practically drooled at the mention of key lime pie.

"Do you mind?"

"Go on. And I'll have a coffee. Decaffeinated, please."

A rat-tat-tat sound started. Flynn and Ace simultaneously glanced at the ceiling.

"Guess the rain's finally started," the waitress said, and scurried off to bring their pie and coffee.

"I was hoping we might escape more foul weather," Ace said. "I'm tired of mucking through soggy fields and getting my truck stuck in a wash."

"It has been an awfully wet spring."

Ace demolished his pie in four bites.

Flynn had no idea where he put it. There wasn't an ounce of fat on him, while she ruthlessly watched every crumb of food she ate in order to maintain her size six figure.

Size *pregnant*, soon.

She should probably enjoy Ace's appreciative glances while they lasted.

He supported her elbow as they left the restaurant. Considerate, without being pushy.

"You want my hat?" he offered.

They waited outside the front door, assessing the pouring rain.

"I won't melt," she said with a laugh.

"You wait here while I get the truck."

He'd no sooner uttered the words when

they heard a loud metallic crunch in the darkness to their right.

"What's that?" Flynn asked, peering through the downpour at the headlights of a compact SUV.

Ace was already in motion, sprinting in the direction of the disabled vehicle.

She followed, holding the flaps of her coat closed around her as she jogged between puddles. Reaching the SUV, she found Ace bent over the open driver's side window.

"Are you sure you're okay?" He had to practically shout in order to be heard above the rain.

"I'm fine. Just embarrassed," came a disembodied female voice.

The door opened and Sierra Byrne stepped out.

Flynn immediately recognized the owner of the diner. She and Sierra had taken exercise classes together off and on through the years.

"Hey, Sierra. Can I help?"

Within seconds, the rain had soaked the young woman. Flynn could feel the dampness penetrating her own coat and ignored the discomfort.

"It's just a fender bender," Sierra insisted. "I mean, I hope it's a fender bender."

They all three inspected the rear of her car, which sat a few inches from the parked mini-van she'd hit. Between the darkness and the rain, it was impossible to discern the damage.

"Do you have a flashlight?" Ace asked Sierra.

"No."

"I do. In my truck." He was off before Sierra could stop him.

Flynn put her arm around Sierra's waist. "You want us to take you to the clinic?"

"Really, I'm okay."

"You're shivering."

"I'm mad at myself. I can't believe I missed seeing that van."

"It was an accident."

Sierra's gaze went to Ace. "I'm glad to see you with Ace. I always thought you two would make a perfect couple."

Flynn felt her flush return, though how that was possible in the midst of a downpour, she wasn't sure. "We're not together. Not like that."

"Too bad."

"We're having a baby."

Where had that come from? Flynn had decided to keep the news to herself, Ace and their families until she'd reached her second trimester and figured out her plans.

"You are?" Sierra's face brightened. "I'm so excited for you. Congratulations."

They were hugging when Ace returned.

"Forget about me," Sierra chided him. "You two go on and celebrate. Flynn told me about the baby," she added when Ace looked confused.

He grinned broadly, like a proud papa. "Thanks. But I'm here, and I have my flashlight, so we might as well take a look." He aimed the beam at Sierra's SUV first, then the van. "Doesn't appear too bad. A couple small dings in the bumpers is all. Easily fixed."

"Darn it." Sierra pouted. "Guess I'd better get back inside and find the owner. Give him my insurance information."

"Want us to go with you?"

"Honestly." She gave him and Flynn a small push. "Get out of here. You're soaked."

They were, and Flynn's teeth were starting to chatter.

Ace hurried her along to his truck with a parting "Be careful" to Sierra.

Opening his passenger side door, he helped

her in, then raced to his side. The rain continued to fall in torrents, making a thunderous noise as it pummeled the truck.

Ace started the engine and turned on the heater. "Better?" he asked when the air finally blew warm.

"A little." Flynn's teeth had yet to cease chattering.

"Take off your wet coat." He was already shrugging out of his jacket. When he finished, he helped her with a sleeve that stubbornly clung to her clothing.

She laid the sopping coat across her lap, which only added to her misery.

"That's not helping." Ace deposited the coat in the back alongside his jacket. He'd yet to put the truck in reverse. "I'd offer you a blanket, but the only one I have is a saddle blanket and it's covered in horse hair."

"I'll be all right." She would, if she could just get warm.

She reached for the seat belt buckle. It slipped from her stiff fingers and was sucked up by the roller.

He bent toward her.

She assumed he was going to buckle her in. Instead, he flipped up the console separating them, put an arm around her shoulders and drew her across the seat to nestle beside him.

Flynn might have protested if not for the sudden warmth flooding her.

"How's that?"

"Good."

They stayed where they were, the rain continuing its assault. They stayed even when the heater had raised the temperature in the truck cab to a lovely, toasty level.

"I think I'm okay now," Flynn said, breaking the silence, which had actually been nice and companionable, and attempting to return to her side of the seat.

Ace didn't release her.

She looked up at him, about to ask if something was the matter.

His dark gaze swept over her face and sent every thought in her mind fleeing, save one.

I'm in big trouble.

A tiny sigh escaped her as he lowered his mouth to hers.

She should push him away, tell him no. This kind of recklessness was exactly what had landed them in the pickle they were today.

Except she didn't push him away. Not when his lips brushed hers, not when his hand reached up to tenderly cradle her cheek, not when he pressed her into the seat and deepened the kiss.

The roar outside filled her ears as Ace's heated kiss filled her senses. Raised her awareness. Sent her spinning. They were no strangers to intimacy, but this, oh, this was different. There was an emotional connection unlike any she'd experienced before. They were linked, by the child she carried, the history they shared, the feelings they had for one another.

Wrapping her arms around his neck, she returned his kiss with matching fervor, wrenching a low, desperate groan from him. It wasn't enough. She placed her right palm over his heart, needing to feel it beat, faster and stronger as their kiss intensified.

Imagine a lifetime of this, a small voice inside her murmured.

She'd have it if she accepted Ace's proposal.

The next instant, sanity returned. Incredible kisses were no reason to get married.

Ace evidently sensed the change and released her. She drew back slowly. His hoarse, unsteady breathing echoed inside the truck cab. She, on the other hand, couldn't draw in air fast enough to feed her starving lungs.

"I'll take you home," he murmured.

"That's probably a good idea." There would be no repeats of past mistakes tonight.

They didn't speak much during the drive. Flynn preferred silence, she wasn't ready to discuss the kiss. She'd rather cherish it for a while longer than analyze their actions or apologize for them. She'd be doing plenty of that later on her own.

Halfway to her father's ranch, Ace's hand reached across the seat for hers. He didn't let go of her until he pulled up in front of the house.

Before she could open her door, he raised her hand to his lips and kissed it.

She sat in stunned silence, staring at him in the murky darkness. Had he really just kissed her hand? Ace Hart?

"Good night, Flynn."

Wordlessly, she got out of his truck and stood in the rain, watching his truck's disappearing headlights.

In all the years they'd known each other, in all the time they'd dated, he'd never been so romantic.

An exquisite shudder coursed through her.

She wasn't just in big trouble, she was heading for disaster.

* * *

"More coffee, honey?"

"Please." Ace held out his mug for a refill, taking another large bite of his breakfast burrito while his mother poured.

"Not so fast," she warned. "You'll give yourself an upset stomach."

He slowed his rate from supersonic to just plain hurried. "I promised Angie I'd stop at the animal shelter this morning after the livestock were loaded. One of her rescue ponies has laminitis."

"Colt and Joshua can oversee the loading."

Colt might if their mother asked him. His brother seemed dead set on avoiding Ace lately, ever since he'd learned about the baby.

"We'll see," Ace mumbled, washing down his burrito with a swallow of coffee.

They were sending a dozen horses and two bulls to the Torrington Rodeo. The rodeo promoters, a husband and wife team, were new clients. Ace's mother was eager to please them, as she'd received bad news earlier in the week when a different contract was canceled during the option period with no real explanation. Their second one.

Normally Ace would accompany the livestock to the rodeo. With the stakes being so high, they didn't need anything to go wrong. But he wanted to stay home to supervise the pasture breeding with Midnight. After nearly a week they were ready to switch out some of the mares.

Colt and Uncle Joshua and the crew Ace had personally selected to travel with them to Torrington were more than up to the task. The rodeo promoters would be happy with the Harts' livestock and their service.

"Gotta run, Mom."

"Wait." She paused from clearing the table. "Do you have a few minutes to talk?"

"If it's about Midnight, he's doing great. Still enamored with that mare of Flynn's. He'll pay attention to the other ones, only as long as he needs to, then he's right back to mooning after Fancy Gal."

"I'm glad the breeding's going well, but it's actually Flynn I wanted to discuss."

Ace sat back down in his chair, finished the last bite of his burrito. When his mother affected *that* tone, he wasn't going anywhere.

"What about Flynn?"

"Have you two made any definite plans yet?"

"No."

"But you're seeing each other."

"Twice in the last week."

Their second outing, to the frozen yogurt shop and public library, hadn't ended the same as their dinner date. Namely, no kiss. Just a hug. Ace would have preferred more. Flynn's keep-away signals had discouraged him from trying.

A shame. Their kiss outside the diner was all he could think about, next to the night they'd spent in her bed.

How could they have dated all those years ago and not kissed or made love with the intensity they did now? What change was responsible?

If he concentrated, he could feel the sensation of her silky skin beneath his fingertips, smell the scent of her floral body wash, taste her lush mouth.

"What did you say?" he asked, realizing he hadn't heard his mother.

"Is Flynn still set on moving to Billings?"

"Yes."

"I wish she wasn't."

"Me, too. I'm working on changing her mind."

"What if I talked to her?"

"I don't know about that. She might think you're interfering. Dig in her heels."

"I suppose." His mother sighed, stared at the window. "I hate the idea of my first grandchild being so far away."

"Tell me about it."

She pressed a hand to her chest and sniffed. "I'm sure it's much worse for you. That was a thoughtless thing to say."

"What's wrong, Mom? You seem sad today."

"It's your brother Tuf."

"Have you heard from him again?"

"No, and that's the problem. One brief phone call to tell me he's been discharged, that he's okay, he'll be in touch soon and not to worry. Nothing about where he is or what he's doing." Her voice hitched. "How am I not supposed to worry?"

"I know." Ace had been so consumed with his own problems, he hadn't noticed the strain in his mother's face and the sorrow in her eyes. "Tuf's a marine. Former marine, anyway. He's capable of taking care of himself."

"You're right. But he's still my little boy. My baby. Why won't he come home?"

Ace was also concerned. It wasn't like Tuf to alienate himself. He'd always kept in regular contact with them up until shortly before his release. Ace was also angry at Tuf—for putting their mother through unnecessary upset and for shirking his responsibilities. Ace had been understanding as long as Tuf was in the Marines, but he was a civilian now. It was long past time for him to come home and take his place in the family business.

One responsibility-challenged brother was bad enough. Ace didn't need two.

"Have you tried calling someone in the Marines?" he asked.

"Even if I could figure out where to start, I'm not sure they'd tell me anything. They're probably not allowed."

"Maybe we should hire someone to track him down."

"Like a private detective?" His mother shook her head. "That's expensive. And Tuf wouldn't like it."

"I don't like what he's doing to us." Ace stood, then bent and kissed his mother on the cheek.

"I'm sorry to pester you and add to your load," she said.

"Don't give it a second thought."

That was what family did, be there for each other. Dinah, Uncle Joshua and his cousins understood. Colt and Tuf just assumed Ace would pick up the slack.

He headed out the kitchen door, started his Polaris and drove to the main barn. Once there, he immersed himself in the job of loading the livestock. It proved useful in fending off his thoughts. Between Flynn, her moving, the baby, the canceled contracts, his mother and his brothers, he had a lot of fending off to do.

Colt wasn't anywhere to be found. So much for his mother's assurance that he'd help them. Gracie and Royce were there along with Uncle Joshua. Oddly enough, Harlan was AWOL, too. The young ranch hand was as dependable as they came.

"Anyone hear from Harlan this morning?" Ace asked.

"No, and that's strange," Gracie answered from inside one of the trailers. She was hosing it out before the horses were loaded.

Ace dialed Harlan's number on his cell phone. He was in no mood for slackers and ready to tear Harlan a new one for being late.

"Hello," a breathy female voice answered, taking Ace momentarily aback.

Then he remembered who he was dealing with and what a ladies' man Harlan was. "Is Harlan there? I need to speak to him."

"He can't come to the phone."

"This is his boss, Aidan Hart. What's wrong?" Ace didn't care that Harlan was typically a good employee. If he was nursing a hangover and lolling around in bed with a woman, Ace was firing him.

"He's asleep."

"Asleep!" At eight in the morning? "Wake him up now. Please," Ace added through gritted teeth.

"I would, but the doctor said not to."

"The doctor?"

"At the emergency room last night. The poor baby has some kind of food poisoning. I don't know what he ate. We were at the Open Range Saloon. He took me dancing." She giggled. "We got these nachos off the happy-hour menu—"

"Is Harlan okay?" Ace didn't care about the dancing and what caused the food poisoning.

"The doctor said he'll be fine. Just needs to rest. The medicine makes him groggy. Guess I should have tried to call you. I had an awful time getting him from the truck into bed. That's not how it usually is." She giggled again.

"Thanks for letting me know. I'll send someone by later to check on him." Ace disconnected, feeling guilty for condemning Harlan before learning the facts. "Where's Colt?" he asked out loud.

The same answer came back as the first time Ace asked the question. No one had any idea.

He dialed his brother's cell phone, relief surging through him when Colt promptly answered.

"Where are you?"

"About halfway to Torrington."

"What! Why aren't you here? We're loading the stock."

"I told you I was going early."

"No, you didn't," Ace snapped.

"I could've sworn."

"Dammit to hell, Colt."

"I'll me—you th—help wi—"

Whatever his brother said was garbled as their reception went from poor to nonexistent.

Ace shoved his phone in his pocket, barely restraining himself from pitching it into the side of the trailer. His energy was better spent readying the horses for transport.

"Something wrong?" Uncle Joshua asked.

"Colt took off early for Torrington. Didn't tell anybody."

"We'll be okay."

"No, we won't. Harlan's sick. Food poisoning. He's on medication."

"That'll leave us one driver short."

"No, it won't. I'll go." He'd stop at Angie's rescue shelter on the way to treat the pony's laminitis.

There were days he'd give his right arm for a veterinarian assistant.

"What about Midnight and the mares?" Uncle Joshua asked.

"Gracie will have to be in charge." She couldn't fill in for Colt, not with two sons at home to watch.

Ace groaned. Taking three days off to attend the rodeo was going to wreak havoc with his schedule—his date with Flynn in particular. But what choice did he have? Hopefully she'd understand.

Just when they were making progress…

Ace cursed his brothers under his breath. How pitiful was it when he could rely more on an employee than family members?

When he next saw Colt and Tuf, he was going to give the both of them a much-needed lesson in priorities.

Chapter 9

Flynn reread the printed email from the University of Montana, then set it down beside her, a sound of discontent escaping her lips.

Her father discovered her several minutes later, still sitting on the front porch swing and rocking idly.

"You're mighty glum," he observed.

"Transferring to the university isn't going to be as easy as I thought. And apparently I should have applied to nursing school last spring. There aren't any current openings."

"Can you still take classes even if you aren't in nursing school?" He sat on the sturdier of the two wicker chairs, easing himself into it with a weary groan.

"Sure. Once I complete the transfer process. Seems there's a problem with that, too. My transcripts are incomplete. I have to contact Billings Community College."

"You'll get it done."

"Yeah, but I'm frustrated. I really wanted to start with an online class or two this summer."

"Well, we may be stuck here a while longer."

"Why? What's happening?"

"Nothing's happening. That's the problem. Haven't had but one serious buyer look at the place, and it's been on the market a while now." He rolled his head from side to side, wincing as he did.

"Hurt yourself?"

"Naw, just sore. Think I might have overdone it."

He'd spent the majority of the day performing minor repairs from the list the real estate agent had given him. According to her, a little fixing up, a little cleaning up, a little sprucing up would improve her father's chances of selling.

"Not many people in the market for a ranch, I guess." Flynn recalled her conversation with Ace on the topic.

"I came down on my price."

And he'd probably have to come down a lot more. "Give it time, Dad."

He smiled. "I could tell you the same thing about school."

"You're right." She smiled back at him. "Are you that anxious to move?"

"Some days, yes. Some days, no. Lived here my whole life. Your grandfather built this entire place board by board."

Flynn felt the same. She'd wake up in the morning, excited about school and her return to Billings. By afternoon, she dreaded leaving Roundup.

And, if she were honest with herself, leaving Ace, too.

It was different before. When she'd headed off to college eleven years ago, she'd been moving toward something. A bright new future. Endless possibilities. Now, despite the excitement of continuing her education and expecting a baby, it seemed as if she was running away, and she couldn't explain why.

"Aren't you and Ace going out tonight?"

Two dates and already her father assumed she and Ace were an item.

"Not anymore. He left yesterday for the

rodeo in Torrington. One of their hands contracted food poisoning. Ace stepped in."

"Don't take it so hard."

"I'm not."

"Really? Because you remind me of that Christmas you were seven and Nora told you there was no Santa Claus."

It was true. She'd been surprised at the depth of her disappointment when Ace had called to cancel. Her annoyance, now that was no surprise. Fair or not, thanks to her ex-husband, Flynn had a low tolerance for men married to their jobs.

"Cut him some slack," her father said. "He didn't stand you up for no good reason. They had a contract to fulfill."

"I'm not mad at him, Dad."

"You think he should have sent someone else in his place."

Kind of, yes. The Harts employed a lot of hands. "I have no idea." She pushed the email aside.

"Ace wants to be with you. He wouldn't have gone to Torrington if he had any other choice."

"That's just it. I want a man who has other choices. Who doesn't live, eat, breathe work."

"It's a date, Flynn. You'll go out with him again this week."

"What if it was more than a date? What if I went into labor or the baby was sick? Would he still run off to some rodeo because an employee called in sick?"

"You can depend on him when it really matters."

Flynn conceded she was probably making a bigger deal out of the canceled date than she should. Blame raging hormones. The tone in Ace's voice had been reminiscent of Paul's, and it struck an old, inharmonious chord in her.

"Maybe you should stay in Roundup. Get an apartment."

"Why wouldn't I move when you do?"

"Ace, for one. And the baby."

"I'm going to college, Dad. There are other nursing schools in Billings." Not affiliated with the university but as good.

"Are you certain being a nurse is what you want?"

"Absolutely." Or was she simply talking herself into it?

He inclined his head at the letter. "Wouldn't hurt anything if you waited until after the baby was born. Give yourself time to enroll in nursing school and straighten out that transcript problem."

"Those are small glitches."

"But you love Ace."

She did. Their dates, under the guise of doing what was best for the baby, were wonderful. Fun and heady. They were also difficult. She'd come home feeling like she was standing on the edge of a precipice, swaying in the ever-changing wind.

He liked her. Desired her. Respected and possibly adored her. He didn't, however, love her in return. And it hurt.

"How I feel about Ace is irrelevant. What matters is how he feels about me."

"He asked you to marry him."

"He did it for the baby."

"That's the excuse he gave you. Ace isn't a man of fancy-schmancy words or romantic gestures. He'll show you he loves rather than tell you."

She thought of last week when he'd kissed her hand before she got out of his truck.

"If he loved me, he'd have sent someone else to the Torrington Rodeo."

"Ace isn't Paul. He's not using work as an excuse to avoid you."

Flynn's eyes stung. The wounds she'd believed healed clearly weren't.

At that moment, her phone beeped. "It's a
text from Ace." She pressed the button and
displayed the message.

How are you? Been thinking of you a lot.

Not fancy-schmancy words by any stretch
of the imagination, but they melted her heart.

"From the look on your face, it must be a
dandy message."

"He's just asking how I am."

And thinking about her.

Could it be? Were his feelings for her
stronger than she'd realized?

Been thinking of you, too, she texted back.

Okay, Flynn admitted it, Ace was trying.
He'd apologized for postponing their date,
brought flowers when he picked her up—tu-
lips, a dozen—and was taking her to a chick
flick.

Of the thirty or forty people in line to
purchase tickets, she estimated he was one
of maybe six guys. The only cowboy. And
he didn't seem to mind, either her choice of
movie or standing out from the crowd.

She didn't mind him standing out, either, or the envious glances being cast her way.

"The movie's had some good reviews," he commented as they stepped ahead.

"You read them?"

"I checked online."

"Preparing yourself for the worst?"

"Not at all." He grinned, a mildly heart-fluttering grin. "I'm glad to be here with you. I don't care what movie we see."

Neither did she.

If he were a little less the perfect date, she'd be better able to resist him.

All the other couples in line were openly affectionate, either holding hands, arms wrapped snugly around each other or standing with their heads bent in whispered conversations. Ace and Flynn didn't touch, they hadn't since he'd kissed her hand.

"Maybe next time we can see an action movie." He dug out his wallet in preparation for purchasing tickets.

"You know, we don't always have to go on dates. We can just hang out. Talk. Go hiking. Horseback riding."

"You're not getting on a horse while you're pregnant."

She laughed, having made the last remark only to get a rise out of him. "Fishing, then."

"I like going on dates with you."

She liked it, too. More than she should.

They were two customers away from the ticket window when Ace's cell phone rang.

Flynn's heart plummeted.

"I'll send this to my voice mail—" He read the caller ID, said, "Sorry," and answered with a brusque, "Ace Hart." After listening for several seconds, he asked, "How bad is she? Can she walk?" Another pause. "That's normal. She's probably in shock. How cold is it in the garage?… Okay, if you can reach her, cover her with a blanket or coat but don't disturb her."

"Is everything all right?" Flynn mouthed. They were almost to the window.

He gave her an apologetic head shake. "I'll be there as quick as I can. No, it's all right. Don't worry." He disconnected. "Flynn, there's been an emergency."

"I could tell."

They stepped out of line and started toward the parking lot. There would be no movie tonight.

Why was she surprised?

"It's a client of mine. The Andersons. Their

son Curt ran over their family dog. The kid's sixteen and just got his license."

"Is the dog all right?"

"They don't know. She can't walk and is hiding under an old table in the garage. She's also bleeding at the mouth."

Flynn's frustration fled upon hearing about the dog's condition. "How's their son?"

"Pretty shaken up but otherwise fine."

"I didn't think you treated dogs."

"I don't, but the Andersons are also friends. You might have heard of them, they raise alpacas."

"I've seen the farm on the outskirts of town."

"It's quite an interesting operation."

They reached Ace's truck.

"Be sure and phone me later," Flynn said. "Let me know how the dog is."

"Actually…"

"What?"

"I hate to have to tell you this, but there's no time to drop you off first."

"You're taking me with you?"

"The Andersons live on the opposite side of town. I hope you don't mind."

"Um…no."

"This could take a while."

"Don't worry about me."

In the three years Flynn and Paul were married, countless last-minute work emergencies had cropped up. Not once did he suggest she accompany him.

"Will it be all right if I go with you?" she asked. "I don't want to get in the way."

"You'll be fine."

Ten minutes into the drive, Ace called the Andersons and received an update on the dog's condition. It remained unchanged. When they pulled into the alpaca farm, Mrs. Anderson was waiting for them in the driveway, wringing her hands.

"Thank you for coming, Ace." Her voice wobbled. "We didn't know what to do or who to call."

"No problem."

"Lovey's over here."

She hurried them to the garage. Flynn blinked at the bright florescent lights.

"Hello, Ace," Mr. Anderson said.

The two men shook hands, and Ace introduced Flynn.

A pale-faced teenage boy—he had to be their son Curt—sat cross-legged in front of an old dining room set. Someone had moved the chairs to the side, creating a pathway to the dog.

She lay beneath an old raincoat, only her nose and muzzle showing. Even at a distance, Flynn could see dark blood caked on the side of the dog's mouth.

The son sprang out of the way. Ace knelt in front of the dog and carefully removed the raincoat.

"Hey, girl."

The dog trembled violently and gazed at him with a woeful expression.

He carefully opened her mouth and pushed her lips aside.

Lovey whimpered and jerked her head from his grasp.

Talking soothingly, he continued the exam, palpating her sides and belly. She tolerated this considerably better, though she panted laboriously.

"I don't detect any internal injuries."

"No?" Mrs. Anderson asked. She waited beside Flynn, her hands still clenched in front of her.

"Then how come she's bleeding?" Curt asked.

Ace peeled back Lovey's lip to show them. "She's cut the inside of her mouth on her teeth, probably happened on impact with the car. It doesn't look bad."

"Thank God." Mrs. Anderson went visibly weak.

"Why can't she walk?" Mr. Anderson asked.

"Let's see what we can find."

With profound gentleness, Ace lifted the dog out from beneath the table and set her on her feet—her three feet. She held her right front paw out in front of her at a painful angle.

Flynn could see now that Lovey was a yellow Lab, with possibly a little German shepherd thrown in for good measure. She demonstrated how she'd earned her name by giving Ace's face a thorough washing.

He chuckled, trying to evade her tongue. "I like you, too, girl."

When he pressed down on her paw, she whined and tried to retreat beneath the shelter of the table.

"Want me to hold her?" Mr. Anderson offered.

"No. She's in mild shock. I don't want to cause her unnecessary distress."

Flynn was impressed with both the compassion Ace showed Lovey and his kind treatment of the Andersons. She'd been fortunate to work with several nurses and doctors at the emergency clinic who possessed the same admirable bedside manner. They were one of the reasons for her wanting to become a nurse.

She hadn't really thought about how a veterinarian interacted with his patients' owners. Most of the vets her father had used over the years were nice but efficient. Not nearly as tenderhearted as Ace.

He'd been every bit as gentle and compassionate with Fancy Gal as with Lovey. It was obvious to anyone he loved his job, his patients and helping to make their owners' lives better.

She longed for the same things herself.

Perhaps they weren't so different after all.

"Flynn. Would you mind bringing me my medical case?" He passed her his keys. "It's in the compartment on the driver's side. Black box with a handle. The small silver key opens the lock. I also need a bottle of antiseptic wash. It's on the bottom shelf, white label. Make sure there's enough gauze and a roll of elastic cohesive bandage in the case. If not, grab a few more."

Flynn hurried to the truck. Opening the side compartment, she quickly located the items Ace needed.

Mrs. Anderson returned at the same time

as Flynn. Apparently she'd been dispatched to fetch a pan of warm water.

Using a bulb syringe procured from his medical case, Ace flushed out Lovey's mouth with the antiseptic wash and cleaned the blood from her muzzle.

"What about her foot?" Mrs. Anderson asked.

"My guess is she's broken two or three toes." He showed the Andersons the raised bumps on Lovey's paw. "I'm going to bind the paw to stabilize and protect it and give her an injection for pain—she'll be in a lot of it from the broken toes and the blow she sustained. She should be okay until Monday morning when you can take her to your regular vet. But I wouldn't recommend waiting any longer."

"She ran out in front of me as I was pulling in the driveway," Curt lamented. "I didn't see her. There was just this awful thud." He cringed.

"Go easy on yourself." His mother squeezed his arm. "What's important is that she's going to be fine."

Ace finished binding the paw. Lovey was visibly relieved when he snipped the tape and released her. She barely noticed the injection he administered.

"Keep her quiet and warm for the next couple days. Make sure she has water available but don't be alarmed if she doesn't drink or eat much. It's normal. Call me if there's any change for the worse."

All three of the Andersons walked Ace and Flynn to his truck where she helped him load the supplies.

"What do I owe you?" Mr. Anderson asked Ace.

"I'll just add the charges on the bill for my regular visit next week."

Mrs. Anderson hugged him warmly. "Thank you again."

"I'll see you Wednesday," Ace said as he and Flynn opened the truck doors. "Let me know what your vet says about Lovey."

When they were back on the road, Ace asked, "You want to try and catch the late show?"

Flynn shrugged. "If you don't mind, I'd rather not."

His features fell ever so slightly. "I'm really sorry about ruining the evening."

"You didn't ruin it at all. I enjoyed going with you to the Andersons'."

"Don't ever take up poker. You haven't the face for it."

"It's true. I really did have fun." She gazed at him earnestly. "What you did for the Andersons, that was nice."

"They're good people."

"You are, too, Ace. A good person and a good vet. I can tell by the way you treated Lovey and Fancy Gal. I never thought being a vet was all that cool until tonight."

He grinned. "If I knew you were interested in my vet practice, I'd show you my clinic rather than take you home."

"Let's go!"

"I was joking."

"I'm not."

"It's getting late." He checked the digital clock on the dashboard.

"Not that late. Come on," she insisted. "I've never seen your clinic."

"Okay." Ace's smile remained in place until they arrived at Thunder Ranch.

He flipped on the lights at the entrance to the main horse barn. The occupants stirred at the disturbance, milling in their stalls and nickering.

"My office is this way." He patted a curious head here and there as they walked down the aisle and past the tack room. Opening a door, he turned on a second light and waited for Flynn to enter first.

She didn't recall what this room had been before its current incarnation. A storage area, perhaps? No more than ten feet by eight feet, it contained a desk, a computer straight out of the stone age, a printer/scanner/fax machine almost as old, shelves filled with numerous medical volumes and reference books, a small refrigerator in the corner with a microwave on top and a four-drawer lateral file.

"This is nice," Flynn observed.

"You really gotta watch that poker face."

"Quit it!"

"It's small." He shrugged. "I don't need much. Not yet."

"Does that computer actually work?"

"I could probably use a new one."

She indicated a door beside the cabinet. "Where does that lead?"

"I'll show you." They went outside. Ace flipped on a third light switch, illuminating two covered pens. A young calf stood in one of them, his huge eyes woefully sad. "This is my hospital ward."

"What's wrong with him?" Flynn went over to the calf, who investigated her fingers with his sticky tongue.

"He's an orphan. His mama died a few days ago."

"Oh, no! What happened?"

"Rattlesnakes. She inadvertently wandered into a nest of them."

"Poor thing." Flynn scratched the calf between the ears. "What are you going to do with him?"

"Try and put him with another cow and calf, see if the cow will accept him. If not, I guess I'll be hand-raising him."

The calf brayed mournfully.

"What's wrong?" Flynn asked.

"He's hungry. He's always hungry."

"Can we feed him?"

"Sure."

They went back into Ace's office where he prepared the calf's formula, pouring the mixture into a huge baby bottle.

The calf brayed louder than before the second they appeared with the bottle.

"Slow down!" Flynn giggled as the calf sucked lustily, emptying the contents in a matter of minutes.

"You're hired," Ace told her when they were done. "But you'll have to come back tomorrow."

"Maybe I will." Flynn realized she was serious. Back inside the office, she asked, "What kind of software do you use for your practice?"

"'Fraid I don't have a very sophisticated system. Spreadsheets, mostly, and those are pretty basic."

"How do you keep track of your patients' histories?"

"A manila file folder." He rested a hand on top of the lateral file.

"Honestly? Ace, you need to update your system. And buy a new computer," she added emphatically.

"I know. I haven't had the time."

"I could help." The words popped out of her mouth before she could stop them, not that she wanted to.

"You would?"

"It's what I do at the clinic. I can't imagine there's much difference."

"You haven't seen my system."

"Let me take a look at it sometime this week. You may not need to make as many changes as you think."

"I'd really appreciate it. And I'll pay you."

"You will not!"

"I can't ask you—"

"You're not asking, I'm offering. And it's something I like doing."

"What about nursing school? Will helping me get in the way?"

"It shouldn't. As it is, I've hit a bit of a road-block."

"A bad one?"

"Nothing I can't resolve. Helping you will give me something to think about other than how long the process is taking."

"I won't say no. I can use an expert."

Pleasure bubbled up inside her.

Soon after that, Ace took Flynn home. The hug and peck on the lips he gave her at the door felt right and natural. Before going inside, she reminded him of her upcoming doctor's appointment.

Her father was still up when she strolled into the kitchen, humming softly.

"You're home early. Have a good time?"

"I did. A really good time." She fixed herself a glass of iced water and told him about her evening with Ace.

"Sounds like fun."

"It was."

The most fun she'd had with Ace in…possibly ever.

What did that say about their evolving relationship?

Chapter 10

"You didn't tell me how the calf was doing."

"Fine." Ace wiped his sweaty palms on the legs of his jeans.

"Did you find a cow to accept him?"

He stared at the door leading to the exam rooms. "Um, yeah. Finally."

"What's wrong?" Flynn asked.

"Nothing."

"You seem kind of on edge today."

"Do I?" He leaned forward in the visitor's chair, feeling his shirt sticking to his back.

"Are you anxious about the ultrasound?"

"A little." He and Flynn had finished with

her exam and were waiting for their turn in the imaging room.

"The doctor said everything appears normal and right on schedule."

"I heard her."

"Then why are you sweating like a pig?"

"I'm excited."

"Talk about a lousy poker face."

"I'm not anxious."

"Are you afraid of doctors? Because you've been like this since we arrived. I thought you were going to pass out during my exam."

"Don't be ridiculous."

"You're a vet. How can a vet be afraid of doctors?"

He exhaled. "I guess I know too much."

"What happened? Did you have a traumatic experience as a child?"

"I broke my arm when I was seven. It didn't heal correctly, so the orthopedic surgeon had to rebreak it."

"That's not so terrible."

"Without anesthesia or painkillers!"

"You poor kid." She patted his hand. "I'll be with you the whole time. I won't let the mean, evil doctor near you."

"I'm supposed to be the one supporting

and comforting you," he said glumly, irritated at himself.

"Is your broken arm why you became a vet?"

"Actually, it was old Doc Pilchard's fault. Remember him? He'd come out to the ranch, let me help him treat the horses and cattle. I'd keep the IV bag raised while he removed an abscessed tooth or reattached a torn ligament."

Next to his dad teaching him to ride and bust broncs, Doc Pilchard's visits to the ranch were some of Ace's fondest childhood memories. The old vet had retired after a lengthy and respectable career, beloved by all.

That was Ace's ambition. He would not end his life like his father, tainting everyone and everything important to him.

"And yet," Flynn said, "you quake at the prospect of being in the room during an ultrasound. There aren't any needles involved, or has no one told you?"

"I hear the gel they use is cold."

"You'll be fine." She squeezed his fingers, her tone soothing rather than ridiculing or patronizing.

When she would have withdrawn her hand,

he held fast. After a few seconds, she relaxed. So did Ace.

A man wearing a lab coat and looking barely old enough to be out of high school stepped into the waiting area and called her name. He escorted them down a chilly hallway to an even chillier room.

"Undress down to your underwear and put on the gown, open in the front," he said, and shut the door behind him.

There was no curtain or privacy screen behind which to change. Ace sat on the only chair in the room and glanced away while Flynn removed her clothes and donned the gown. When she finished she sat on the edge of the exam table, holding the gown closed.

"Cold?" Ace asked.

"A bit. What about you?"

"Great."

"Don't tell me all that shaking is from nerves."

Luckily the imaging technician returned, relieving Ace of having to respond.

"Lie back," he instructed Flynn, and went about preparing for the ultrasound.

Before long he was gliding the probe over Flynn's still flat belly. He stopped, pointed to a blurry image on the monitor beside her.

"There. See?"

The image became clearer as he held the probe in place.

"Yes!" Flynn radiated delight.

Ace saw only a white-and-gray swirl.

No, wait! There was a shadowy oblong shape in the center of the screen and within it, a small spot pulsated.

"That's your baby's heart." The tech smiled.

The shape slowly took form. A head. Body. The beginnings of arms and legs.

"Look here." The tech moved the probe, and a small ghostlike face suddenly appeared amid the swirl.

Flynn said something. Ace couldn't hear her over the roaring in his ears.

This tiny human being was his child. Alive and thriving. Soon he'd be holding his son or daughter in his arms, picking a name, showing him or her off to his family, walking ten feet off the ground.

"It's too early to determine the sex," the doctor said.

"I don't care," Ace blurted, unable to tear his gaze away from the monitor.

"So, you won't mind if I hope for a boy?" Flynn asked.

He reached for her hand and gripped it

tightly. "Boy, girl, one of each, it doesn't matter."

"One of each!" Flynn stared at the monitor. "There is only one baby, right?"

The tech moved the probe. "Just one. The right size for nine weeks and the right stage of development. Congratulations."

Flynn sighed happily.

"Baby's first pictures," the tech said, pressing buttons on the ultrasound machine. A moment later an image slid out, the thin paper curling. Then another, and another. "Here you are." He handed the images to Flynn.

Ace leaned in close for a better look. They were the most amazing pictures he'd ever seen.

He and Flynn were still staring when the tech left and the doctor returned. She recited a list of instructions to which Flynn nodded and mumbled a reply. When they were alone again, Ace laid his palm lovingly on Flynn's stomach.

"It's real, isn't it? We're having a baby."

She covered his hand with hers, her eyes misting. "Yes, we are."

"I won't let you down. I'll be a good father." He'd be a good husband, too, if she'd accept his proposal.

Nodding and swallowing, she gave Ace the images and sat up.

"Can we get copies of these on the way home?" he asked.

"Sure."

This time Ace didn't have to glance away while Flynn dressed, he was still transfixed by the images. How could something this tiny grow into a baby? Into a full grown person?

"Would you be upset if we had a girl?" he asked.

Flynn finished dressing and came over. "All I want is a healthy baby."

"I'll be better during the next doctor appointment."

"You don't have to come every time."

He stood. "Yes, I do. I promised I'd be here for you."

"As long as you don't faint in the delivery room."

"Thanks for the vote of confidence."

"Want me to take those?" She held out her hand.

Ace was hesitant to relinquish the images. He did, and she slipped them into her oversize purse.

When she started toward the door, he reached for her. "Flynn, wait."

"What is it?" She gazed at him, her expression curious.

"I meant what I said. I love our baby and can't wait to be a dad."

Her vivid blue eyes dimmed. "Ace..."

"Don't bring up that you're moving. That nothing's changed. Not today."

"All right, I won't," she answered quietly.

Ace watched her closely as she stopped at the front desk and set her next appointment, waited for the elevator, walked across the parking lot.

He was determined as ever not to give up, on her or them.

Now that he'd seen his child's face, watched its speck of a heart beating wildly, he had more reason than ever to fight for Flynn and the life they could have if she'd just give them a chance.

Flynn sat on the corner of her bed, staring at her copies of the ultrasound images. She and Ace had visited the one-hour photo shop on the way home from the doctor's office and got copies made—for him, his mother and Flynn's sister.

Ace was so excited, like a kid with his first puppy. He'd described the images to the store clerk, a middle-aged man who listened with surprising patience. The man had gone on to tell her and Ace about his own experiences with his wife during her pregnancies.

Flynn had to admit, Ace was cute and his reaction touching.

It made hurting him all the worse.

And she would hurt him, terribly, when she moved. There had to be some way she could minimize the blow.

Yeah, right. All the pictures in the world couldn't replace being with your child.

"Anybody home?" Her father's greeting echoed through the house a scant second after Flynn heard the kitchen door open and close. He'd been gone the entire morning, meeting with a potential buyer for their remaining bucking stock.

"Hey, Dad," Flynn called, taking the ultrasound images with her to show him.

He was in the kitchen, fixing himself a plate of leftover lasagna. "Aren't you working today?"

"Evening shift. I go in at four." She held out the images. "I went to the doctor today. Ace came with me."

Her father tilted the various sheets toward

the overhead light to see better. "Well, well. This is…what is this? A baby?"

"Here." She pointed to the head.

He uttered, "Ah!" in that tone people used when they pretended to understand what the other person was talking about.

"The picture's a little fuzzy."

"No, I can see." He grinned but, like frequently of late, it faltered. "My newest grandchild."

"Ace says he wants a girl. I'd like a boy."

"One of you is going to get your wish." Her father sat down at the table with his reheated lunch.

"How'd your meeting go?" she asked.

"He's interested. We have to agree on a price."

His lackluster smile faded completely.

Flynn's concern escalated. "Are you really ready to retire? You can still change your mind."

"I'm tired of running rodeo stock, of maintaining this place. It's a demanding life. One fit for someone younger than me."

"I agree it's hard. What else are you going to do?" Her father was only fifty-seven. Hardly old enough to don a cardigan sweater, plunk down in a rocking chair on her sister's front porch and while away the hours.

"Play with my new grandchild."

"Much as I know you'd both enjoy that, it's not enough to keep you busy."

"I'll probably look for a job." He pushed aside his half-eaten lunch. "There has to be something in Billings I can do. Hardware store or one of those home improvement warehouse stores. I'm pretty handy when it comes to tools and remodeling."

Funny, she hadn't thought about it before. Both she and her father were about to embark on career and lifestyle changes, hers infinitely more exciting.

"Any more nibbles on the ranch?" she asked.

"A couple's supposed to come by this weekend."

"You don't sound too enthused."

"The real estate agent already told me they can't afford to pay what I'm asking."

"Then why are you bothering with showing them the ranch?"

"No harm in it. And we can always negotiate on the price if they're serious." He scraped his plate clean and loaded it into the dishwasher along with his fork.

Flynn noticed the slump of his shoulders, heard the dejection in his voice. "You okay, Dad?"

"I'm tired is all. Didn't sleep good last night."

She suspected his weariness stemmed from more than insomnia. The selling of the ranch, the getting out of the business started by her grandfather, the economic recession, were having an effect on him and his frame of mind. She was no expert on depression, but she'd recently begun suspecting her father might be suffering from it.

Convincing him to see a doctor or counselor would be next to impossible. He'd insist he was fine and dandy and didn't need any headshrinker.

"You know," she said in a cheerful voice, "there is something you could do in Billings."

"What's that?"

"Date."

At least she got a chuckle out of him.

"Can't imagine any woman interested in going out with me."

"Why not? You're handsome. In good shape. Have all your hair—mostly—and all your teeth."

This time his chuckle rang with genuine mirth.

"It's not that far-fetched, Dad."

"Just where would I meet these women interested in a man with all his own hair and teeth?"

"An online dating website?"

That earned her a belly laugh.

"Why not? Lots of people do it. I read somewhere that a third of couples in long-term relationships these days met online."

"I think I'll leave the dating to you and Ace."

She went to the fridge and raided it. Carrying an armful of fresh vegetables to the counter, she started separating and washing them. "I'm fixing myself a salad to take to work. Want one for later?"

"You're ignoring me."

"I'm not. Ace and I aren't dating."

"What would you call it? And, yes, I will have a salad for later if you're offering."

Flynn broke off a large chunk from the head of lettuce. "We're trying to get along so that when the baby comes we'll have a strong and healthy relationship."

"Since when is going to dinner and the

movies and helping him with his vet practice necessary for *getting along?*"

Since when was kissing in the rain necessary?

What would her father say if he knew about that?

"He's going to be brokenhearted when you leave," her father said, giving voice to her earlier thoughts.

She stopped chopping lettuce. "You're right. Maybe I should quit seeing him. Seeing him as much, anyway. I'd hate giving him false hopes."

"He's courting you, you know."

"What? No!"

"Trying to win you over."

"Where did you get such a crazy idea?"

"It's obvious."

She began slicing the tomatoes, rather forcefully.

Ace courting her? Oh, God, he was. She'd been blind not to see it.

"You gonna dice those tomatoes or pulverize them?"

"Huh?" She looked down at the mess on the cutting board.

This courting thing couldn't continue. She had to put an end to it.

The problem was, she liked spending time with Ace, liked helping in his office, liked going on patient calls with him. If she were to examine her own motives, they would probably fall considerably short of innocent.

"He might not be the only one broken-hearted when you leave."

Was her father a mind reader?

More reason than ever to quit seeing Ace so much.

"Want some chicken in your salad?"

"Flynn, honey, I think you should reconsider moving. And Ace's proposal."

She set the knife down.

"You could do considerably worse than him."

"That's no reason to get married, Dad."

"You have a good job here."

"I have a job I like but pays mediocre and has zero potential for advancement. Not unless I return to college and earn my bachelor's degree."

"You have friends here."

"I'll have you and Nora in Billings."

"What are you afraid of?"

"Nothing." *I'm afraid of being married to a man who doesn't love me as much as I love him.*

"Being a single parent isn't easy. Believe me." Her father returned to the table, dropped tiredly into a chair. "As little trouble as you and Nora gave me, I had a lot of rough years after your mom left."

"Why did she leave?" Flynn had asked that question before, of both her parents, though not for a very long time. Her dad's answer always came across as rehearsed and censored. As if he was afraid she couldn't handle the truth.

Her mother's answer, however, was painfully honest. She hadn't been ready for marriage or a family.

Did not being ready make it okay to discard your children like an old pair of shoes that went out of fashion?

Ace may be a little bossy and pushy, but at least he'd stepped up and assumed responsibility.

"I'd say she fell out of love," her father replied, "except I'm not sure she ever was in love to begin with. Not with me."

"Are you saying there was another man?" Flynn abhorred the idea of her mother being unfaithful. It would, however, explain a lot.

"You should ask her why she left."

The answer must be yes.

"If you're worried about affecting my relationship with her, don't be." Flynn put both salads in plastic storage containers and placed them in the refrigerator. "There isn't much of a relationship to affect."

"I'd change that if I could. Your mother has her faults, but she's always loved—"

"If you're going to say she always loved me and Nora, save your breath. It's not true."

"She loves you the best she knows how."

Big deal.

"I'm thankful to Mom," Flynn said. "She's taught me a lot. About what kind of parent not to be, about what kind of marriage not to have."

"The success of a marriage doesn't depend entirely on one person. I made mistakes, too."

"Like letting her go?"

"I'm sorry to say this, but I don't think that was a mistake. For any of us."

"Oh, Dad." Flynn went over and hugged him, then sat down beside him. What courage it must have taken for him to admit that.

"I didn't make it easy for her to love me. She always wanted more than Roundup could offer. I wasn't about to leave the ranch or my parents or my hometown."

"Why did you two get married?" Flynn knew from the date of her parents' wedding and her sister's birthday, it hadn't been a necessity.

"I pleaded with her. Made promises. Tried the best I could to sweep her off her feet."

"Kind of like Ace is doing with me."

"He's trying to show you the good life you and he can have. I bought your mother's affections with exorbitant gifts and trips I couldn't afford. She said yes, thinking it would be like that always. And, of course, it wasn't."

He turned away. Not before Flynn caught the sorrow in his eyes.

More than twenty years had passed and her mother's abandonment still haunted him.

"You loved her."

"I did, even if I wasn't quite sure of the commitment involved."

"Exactly my point, Dad. Ace doesn't love me. I couldn't bear ending up like you and Mom. And I certainly don't want to repeat my own mistake with Paul. Having two people walk out on me is more than enough, thank you."

"Just because he hasn't said the words? Ace isn't demonstrative."

"I need to hear them. I'm not going through my life, always doubting my husband's feelings for me."

"I'm sorry." Her father patted her cheek. "I never realized how much your mom and I messed you up. I'd say being with her was a mistake, but then I wouldn't have you and Nora. Nothing is more important to me than my daughters."

"I feel exactly the same about my baby."

"Tell that to Ace."

"I can't." Flynn rose. "You should have seen his face during the ultrasound. He said he loved our baby. Not me, our baby. And the look on his face… Ace *is* demonstrative. And the man I marry will look at me like I'm the sun and the moon, and he'll tell me every day how much I mean to him. I won't settle for less."

Chapter 11

Ace had yet to meet a horse that didn't love grain. He'd barely closed the pasture gate behind him when the mares started the long walk toward him, recognizing the buckets he carried and anticipating the treat contained within. He dumped the cracked corn into the feed trough, the swishing sound it made prompting several of the mares to break into a trot.

Fancy Gal might love Midnight, but she wasn't adverse to leaving him in the dust for a few mouthfuls of corn.

Ace took a moment to examine the mares, circling them as they ate. To his vast relief, none showed any signs of injury as a result of breeding with Midnight. The stallion was behaving himself.

Speaking of which... Midnight stomped his front hoof in protest at being ignored. His harem paid him no heed.

"Haven't you learned by now how fickle females can be?" Ace asked.

Midnight snorted and tossed his head.

He wanted some corn, too, but wouldn't venture near Ace. Not without incentive—which Ace removed from his shirt pocket.

The carrot gleamed brightly in the afternoon sunlight.

"You got ahold of the mares?" Ace said to Gracie.

She'd followed him into the pasture, slipping halters on the five mares while they polished off the corn.

"We're good to go."

And they did go, back toward the gate. Gracie resembled the Pied Piper, only she led horses instead of mice, first three and then two. She was met by Royce, who helped her tie the mares to the fence railing outside the pasture.

There would be no distractions for Midnight.

"It's just you and me, boy." Ace held out the carrot. There were several more in his shirt pocket. "No need to be shy."

Eventually the horse approached, his steps plodding. Indeed, the condition of his hooves was one reason Ace had committed himself to making progress today. Midnight needed his old shoes removed and his overgrown hooves trimmed.

If Ace didn't tame the horse soon, he'd have no choice but to tranquilize and restrain Midnight. That wouldn't be pleasant for any of them, including the farrier.

Ace snapped the carrot in half, holding the two pieces at arm's length.

Midnight's ears pricked forward.

"Come on, boy, carrots are your favorite."

Ace had tried a variety of treats. Midnight liked them all, but he was fondest of carrots.

Head hanging in defeat, he covered the last few feet, arched his neck and moved his lips in a grabbing motion.

"Not yet." Ace withdrew the carrot. "You have to come closer."

Midnight jerked back, indignation blazing in his black eyes. It didn't last. He quickly succumbed to temptation and took another step forward.

Ace contained his excitement. This was the closest Midnight had voluntarily ventured to anyone except Gracie.

When the horse was finally within touching distance, Ace rewarded him with the carrot half. While he was occupied eating, Ace tentatively stroked the side of Midnight's large head.

The horse reacted as if prodded with a hot poker and promptly bolted.

Ace stood statue still. Eventually Midnight calmed and approached again, not taking nearly as long. When Ace gave him the other carrot half, he tolerated a light petting on the neck, his hide twitching, his eyes saucer wide.

"That's it. Good boy."

Slowly, Ace removed another carrot from his shirt pocket. Midnight immediately swiped it up. He was too busy savoring the tidbit to notice Ace's hand move to his shoulder and chest.

Excitement coiled inside Ace, threatened to explode. He hadn't been able to touch Midnight since the auction.

"I'll buy a whole truckload of carrots if that's what it takes."

He fed Midnight the last one, assuming

the horse would desert him the second he realized no more treats were forthcoming.

Only he didn't.

He stayed and let Ace continue to pet him with slow, easy strokes. After a few minutes, Ace stopped, only to have the horse bump his arm.

Ace's pulse jumped. Now, *this* was progress.

"You want more?" Ace took a chance and scratched Midnight's nose. "You're not such a tough guy after all," he said when the horse blew lustily.

Unfortunately, the moment came to an abrupt end. Ace's mother neared the fence. The second Midnight spied her, he twisted away and galloped to the other side of the pasture, bucking and kicking.

The mares, still tethered, started fussing. They were rodeo horses, after all, and wanted in on the fun.

"Cut 'em loose," Ace told Gracie and Royce.

Within minutes the tiny herd was frolicking in the pasture, Midnight and Fancy Gal reunited and running side by side.

Ace returned to the gate, shutting it behind him.

"Aidan!" his mother gushed. "I saw you and Midnight. That was impressive! Congratulations."

"I'd hoped to be further along by now." He had, but that didn't diminish his pride at his accomplishments.

"At this rate, you'll get there in no time."

"What brings you here?"

"I have some thoughts on the cattle drive tomorrow."

The month of May marked the official start of horse breeding season at Thunder Ranch. It was also when the recently born calves were vaccinated, dewormed, examined and, if necessary, treated. Tomorrow the ranch hands, headed by Uncle Joshua, would be riding the Harts' remaining unleased range, rounding up the cattle and driving them to the holding pens in the south hundred acres. It was a monumental job that would take, at minimum, two full days to complete. The entire family would be on board to assist.

After some last-minute conferring with Ace and his mother, Gracie and Royce headed off to prepare for the morning.

"You going to be home for dinner tonight, or do you have plans with Flynn?"

Ace and his mother began strolling toward the barn. "Not tonight."

Ace would have liked nothing better, but she'd flatly refused his invitation.

"Aren't things going well with you two?"

His scowl must have given him away. "They were. At least, I thought they were. Something's changed the last couple of days."

"Be patient with her. It's paying off with Midnight."

"What if her father sells the ranch? He's had a few interested buyers looking at the place. And he's finalized a deal for his remaining livestock."

Flynn hadn't mentioned the deal to Ace, she didn't need to. Rodeo contracting was a small world and news traveled fast.

"Even if he sold the ranch tomorrow, you'd still have a month or two before the escrow closed."

They reached the barn. Ace held open the door to his office for his mother. Inside, he cranked on a small window air-conditioning unit to clear out the stuffiness. Spring in Montana had arrived, and the days were growing warmer and warmer.

"That's better." She waved a hand as if to fan herself.

He plunked down at his desk, his mother in the chair opposite him. For the first time that day, he noticed her face. It was drawn and paler than usual and there were dark circles beneath her eyes. She also moved as if she carried a heavy sack strapped to her back.

"You doing okay, Mom?"

"Nothing a glass of cold water and a few minutes with my feet up won't cure."

"You look more than tired."

Ever since Tuf's cryptic phone call, she'd had nights when she paced the halls rather than slept. Ace had lost count how often he awoke to the sound of her footsteps padding down the stairs or banging cabinets in the kitchen as she fixed herself a cup of tea.

"How are you sleeping?"

"Okay for the most part."

She was exaggerating and they both knew it.

"Are you worried about Tuf?"

"I worry about all my children."

"Why me?"

"You work too hard. You've taken this new business to heart, which is wonderful. But it's not your responsibility entirely. You need to delegate."

"To who? Colt? When he's not working he's off rodeoing. And most of the hands are putting in overtime as it is."

"Then cut back. You're going to be a father soon."

"Which is why I'm working my tail off. Babies aren't free."

"You have to find a way to balance work and a personal life. Would it really be so terrible if we didn't put Midnight out to stud?"

Ace was aghast. "That's the whole reason we bought him. He has to earn his keep. As it is, we're not taking in the stud fees we'd planned."

"We'll have at least twenty foals next spring from our mares."

"That's a drop in the bucket compared to what he could be doing." Ace felt his blood pressure elevate and forced himself to relax. "You've seen the numbers, what our projected revenue could be. We have to establish Midnight as a proven breeder. Rehabilitate him enough to hand breed him to clients' mares."

"You're right, of course." She slumped in her chair.

"I apologize, Mom. I didn't mean to lecture." Ace smiled.

His mother didn't. "You're passionate about the business. I admire and appreciate that."

"What about Colt has you concerned, other than his chronic aversion to responsibility?"

His mother sighed. "Don't be too hard on him."

Ace didn't think he was hard enough.

"Something's bothering him lately."

"He's been gone more than usual." Ace recalled his brother's strange reaction to the news Flynn was expecting. Could there be a connection?

"I can't help thinking he's wrestling with something big."

"I wish he'd wrestle with it at home. We really could use him." Ace could use him.

"Please don't lose faith. Colt's not that different from you."

"Are you joking? We couldn't be more different!"

"Not when it comes to being disappointed and hurt by your father. Tuf and Dinah, too, for that matter. We've each of us responded in our own way to his drinking. You take on too much responsibility as a result. Colt takes on too little. Tuf left altogether."

"I should have realized Dad had a problem. That he was making bad financial decisions."

"You were away at college and vet school."

"I came home every month."

"I didn't notice, either. We choose to see what we want when it comes to the people we love."

Like his brothers?

His mother's observation sat like a lead ball in Ace's stomach. "Colt needs to grow up. Pull his weight around here."

"Maybe we just need to figure out what motivates him. Flynn, too."

"I'd give anything for the answer to that. She's warm one day, cold the next."

"Being pregnant isn't easy."

"This is more than being pregnant."

He hadn't asked her to marry him again or to reconsider moving. Both topics were guaranteed to trigger a negative reaction.

"Everything was great until after the ultrasound."

"What did you say to her?"

"Nothing I haven't before. That I'd be there for her and the baby."

"Hmm." Now that they were on a different subject than his father and brothers, his mother looked better. Less stressed. "Since you can't pinpoint what went wrong, pinpoint what went right."

Ace raised his brows. "How do you mean?"

"What were you doing when she seemed to be having the best time?"

Ace didn't have to think twice. "When we went to the Andersons and treated their dog. She said she really enjoyed seeing me at work and helping me."

His mother's eyes sparked. "Ask her to go with you on another call."

"I don't have anything scheduled until next Tuesday, and I'm tied up for the next two days vaccinating the calves."

"There you go."

"What? Are you suggesting I ask her to help with the vaccinating?"

"Why not?"

"She's pregnant. It's grueling work. Hot and dirty."

"Just to watch, then."

He opened his mouth to protest, then reconsidered. "She does like animals. No." He shook his head. "It's a crazy idea."

"Sometimes the craziest ideas are the best. What have you got to lose? Unless you want to wait until next Tuesday."

He definitely didn't want that.

With a philosophical shrug, he pulled out his cell phone and called Flynn. After saying hello and asking how she was feeling, he mentioned the calves. "I know it's late notice, but I was wondering if you'd like to come to the ranch the day after tomorrow and...help me. We'd have to get an early start."

"I'd love to!"

"You would?"

"What time should I be there?"

He almost fell off his chair. "Um, seven. Wear old clothes."

His mother smiled smugly at him from across the desk.

"Okay. I'll see you then." He disconnected, still not quite believing what had just happened.

"See?" His mother nodded approvingly. "You just needed to find the right motivation."

Now, if only he could find the right motivation to convince Flynn to remain in Roundup and marry him.

Up until today, Flynn had experienced very little morning sickness. Then again, she hadn't been tossed around the front seat of

Ace's pickup truck like a sneaker in a clothes dryer.

"Can you drive a tiny bit slower?"

He glanced her way. "You want to stop for a rest?"

"No, no." She refused to reveal how truly nauseated she felt. He might turn around and take her home, and she was determined to help him vaccinate the calves.

"I'll be okay once we get there." Which would hopefully be soon.

The day was spectacularly gorgeous. A vivid blue sky lay suspended above rolling green hills. In the distance, elk grazed. Beyond them the mountains rose up, their still snowcapped tips buried in the clouds.

Flynn had been cooped up all week. When she wasn't at the clinic or helping her dad finalize the company books, she was on the phone with Billings Community College and the University of Montana resolving her transcript problem or online researching prenatal care. She'd resisted going into town in order to avoid Ace, his family and their mutual friends.

It was one thing for her and Ace to spend time together for the sake of their child. Quite another to be romantically involved.

People looked at her, at *them,* with the same knowing glances her father frequently cast in her direction.

That wasn't all. Flynn had begun to secretly hope for more from Ace—an admission, a confession, an indication—and that was dangerous. Might as well tape a break-me sign over her heart.

Which left her to wonder where exactly accompanying him to vaccinate the calves fit.

Not a date, that was for sure.

She was assisting him with his job, like when she'd updated his spreadsheets and reorganized his files last week.

The novelty of that still amazed her. Work had never been anything she and her ex-husband shared, other than discussing their respective days over dinner.

Some of the nurses at the clinic complained that they could *never* work alongside their spouses or partners, the strain would surely end their relationships.

The few times that Flynn had helped Ace went smoothly. Enjoyably. No strain whatsoever.

That might change, however, after spending six or seven straight hours with him. Like today.

"I'm surprised you agreed to come along," he said.

"It's just too beautiful to stay indoors." She winced as they went over another bump on the road and pressed a hand to her roiling stomach. "Plus, I needed a break."

"Been busy?"

She nodded, then instantly regretted it, the motion causing her nausea to escalate. "I finally got accepted into the University of Montana."

"Good for you!"

"Even though I can't enroll in nursing school until the spring, I was happy. Then, I started applying for a student loan."

"Uh-oh."

"They're drowning me in paperwork. I no sooner submit one piece of information and they want another. They actually asked for my dad's last tax return. My dad's! Because I live with him. Isn't that an invasion of privacy or something?"

"Hang in there." His tone was genuinely supportive and sympathetic. "It'll be worth it."

She smiled weakly. To be honest, the lengthy

process was wearing her down, and she'd lost most of her initial enthusiasm. For nursing school, not broadening her horizons or finding a more rewarding career. She'd even gone so far as to check into related professions, including respiratory therapy and physical therapy.

Maybe being pregnant had something to do with her waning interest. She couldn't recall ever being so tired.

Ace, and leaving him when she moved, certainly wasn't the reason. Absolutely not. Impossible.

"Sit tight," he said, "we're almost there."

There was the south end of Thunder Ranch and the cattle operation. Barns, pens, trailers and chutes came into view. A dozen trucks and just as many cowboys on horseback had already arrived.

"Busy place." Flynn peered out the window, the low, long braying of cattle growing louder as they approached.

"There's a lot more to vaccinating calves than you think."

"Practically all my life living here, and I've never participated in a cattle roundup."

"Sorry to disappoint you, but the cattle

were mostly rounded up yesterday. The men are going after a few strays today."

"Too bad."

"Next time you can go along."

Much as she'd have liked to attribute the nervous tingling in her tummy to morning sickness, Flynn couldn't. It was pure Ace and that disarming smile of his.

"I don't suppose it's the same as in those old Westerns on TV. Head 'em up, move 'em out and all that," she joked.

"Not exactly. We use trucks."

A shame. She could easily imagine Ace on horseback, herding the cattle to... She squinted. A large corral, from what she could tell.

"It used to take a full week to vaccinate and deworm all the calves when we were running five thousand head." He parked the truck beside a similar one bearing the Thunder Ranch bucking horse logo. "We'll probably finish in a day and a half."

"How do you feel about that?" She opened the door and hopped out, meeting Ace at the side of the truck.

"About finishing in a couple of days?"

"About only running a few hundred cattle instead of thousands. I mean, you grew up raising cattle. That was your family's livelihood. Their heritage."

"It's been a change."

He opened the side compartment on his truck and removed a large plastic case, along with a smaller cardboard box which he handed to her.

"But not a bad one," he continued. "I like practicing veterinarian medicine."

"More than breeding horses?"

They walked toward a group of pens where a half-dozen ranch hands, including Beau and Duke, were sorting the calves, checking their ear tags and noting the numbers on a clipboard. The mamas weren't happy at being separated from their babies and made their objections known with loud vocal protests.

"For me, horse breeding goes hand in hand with veterinarian medicine. Especially once we incorporate artificial insemination into our program."

The plastic tote obviously wasn't as heavy as it appeared, for Ace carried it with ease.

"You think you'll get to that point? Where you're shipping semen across the country?"

"I can't settle for anything less. Not if we're

going to be successful and make money. That loan we took out won't pay itself down."

Flynn liked chatting with Ace about the ranch and his practice and their breeding program. It was a side of him unfamiliar to her. They'd both been focused on school when they dated and residing in Billings. They'd go home on weekends. Separately. John Hart and Flynn's father were at the height of their rivalry then.

"What about you?" Ace asked. "Your life is changing, too. Returning to school is a huge step."

He didn't mention moving. Neither did she.

"School and a baby, too."

His expression turned serious. "Be careful you don't overextend yourself."

"We've already talked about this," she insisted. "I'm starting out a part-time student. Two classes tops."

He set the plastic case down. "I meant today. Vaccinating the calves."

"Oh. Sorry." She bit her lower lip. "I'll take frequent rest breaks, I promise."

"Stay away from the pens and chutes. Cattle can be just as unpredictable as bucking horses and just as dangerous."

As they set up their station, Ace was greeted by his uncle Joshua who updated him on their progress so far.

"What exactly does vaccinating and deworming the calves involve?" Flynn asked when he was finished.

"We drive the calves one at a time from the pen down that narrow chute and into the headgate."

"Headgate?"

"Over there." He pointed to a large metal contraption that stood at least five and a half feet tall and appeared to be operated by a series of levers.

She grimaced and rubbed her throat. "Looks uncomfortable."

"Actually, it's not uncomfortable at all. The calves will raise a fuss for sure, but it is the safest, gentlest and most effective way to restrain them while giving them injections."

Flynn was fascinated. "Can I help?"

He laughed. "You're not running calves down the chute."

Protesting would get her nowhere. "There must be something I can do."

"How handy are you with a syringe?"

"I want to be a nurse, remember?"

"Good." He opened the lid of the plastic

box, revealing a supply of syringes and bottles of clear liquid. "Let me show you how. I need about a hundred of them filled."

She picked up a syringe, eyed the needle beneath the protective cap. "It's huge! Those poor calves."

"It won't hurt. Not any more than when you get a flu shot."

"Hmm." Flynn remained unconvinced.

"Squeamish?"

"Please, don't insult me." Her queasy stomach betrayed her by choosing that moment to lurch.

"I can get Gracie to help me."

"Not on your life." Flynn squared her shoulders and stuck out her chin. "Show me what I need to do."

Chapter 12

"Flynn," Joshua Adams CALLED, attempting to hold a calf steady while reading the ear tag. "Do you have this one?" He recited the number.

She ran down the list on her clipboard, flipped pages and checked off the calf. "Got it."

Having filled all the syringes, she'd been given the task of logging each calf as it was sent down the chute to the headgate.

According to her check marks, they were better than halfway done. A lot of calves and a lot of hard work. Flynn was sweating profusely, and she hadn't labored a fraction as hard as Ace, his uncle, cousins and the ranch hands.

She was also having a thoroughly grand time.

The physically intensive labor was made easier by a friendly camaraderie among the participants. More than once she found herself the brunt of a good-natured jest, and she laughed along with everyone else.

Her attention was diverted as the next calf trotted down the chute, bawling at the top of its lungs. Gracie closed the headgate and before the calf quite knew what was happening, Ace had administered the injection and dewormer.

"Hold on, little fellow." Gracie scratched the calf on the forehead. "Almost done."

Ace conducted a quick exam. "Wait a second," he said when Gracie would have released the lever and freed the calf.

Ace knelt down.

Flynn understood the purpose of restraining the calf when it suddenly kicked out with a hind leg. Luckily, the potential blow missed Ace by a good two feet.

"Flynn," he called. "Bring me the Biozide Gel."

She grabbed the jar from his medical case

and brought it to him. Over the course of a few hours she'd learned the names of almost every item in his case.

"Is he hurt?"

"Nothing much." Ace applied the gel to a small nick on the calf's chest. "Probably got into a tussle with one of his buddies."

"Boys will be boys." Gracie winked at Flynn. "Have two of them myself. Twelve and fourteen."

Flynn imagined her son, a miniature version of Ace, roughhousing with his friends on the Harts' large front lawn or swimming in their backyard pool. Probably the way Ace had roughhoused and swam with his brothers when he was young.

Then she imagined her son in an apartment in Billings—which was probably where she'd be living because she couldn't afford much more on her income, not while she attended school.

Those play sessions at the Harts' would be during the weekends when Ace had their son.

Unless they had a girl, like Ace wanted, then it would be tea parties.

Nah. With Ace for a father, she'd probably be tough as any boy.

"Lunch is here," one of the hands hollered, rubbing his hands together in anticipation.

"Finally," Gracie exclaimed, releasing the calf so that it could be returned to its mother. "I'm starving."

Flynn was, too. Her nausea had disappeared not long after starting work. So, she now noticed, had her fatigue.

The truck carrying their lunches pulled up and Sarah Hart emerged.

"Come and get it!"

Four hungry men beat her to the rear of the truck and began unloading the ice chests.

"You ready?" Ace asked Flynn.

"More than ready." She helped him close up the medical case.

Lunch consisted of sandwiches, fat dill pickles, individual bags of potato chips, cold drinks and homemade brownies for dessert.

Flynn sat on the lowered tailgate of Ace's truck, removed her ball cap and ate like a starved animal, licking the brownie crumbs off her fingers when she was done.

"Finished already?" Ace joined her, the other half of his sandwich still in his hand, his bag of chips unopened.

"Lightweight," she muttered.

"Do you mind?" He nodded at the tailgate.

In reply, she scooted over.

"I guess you're eating for two." The truck rocked unsteadily as he made himself comfortable.

"That's my story, and I'm sticking to it."

"Want my brownie?"

"No, thanks." She'd already had two. "I'm glad you invited me today."

"I should have warned you how labor-intensive it was going to be."

"Doesn't bother me."

"You taking it easy?"

"I feel fantastic. Lately I've been getting tired and can hardly keep my eyes open. Today I'm the Energizer Bunny."

"Wait till tonight. Then you'll be tired."

"If I'd known how much fun your job is, I'd have come with you sooner."

"You're welcome to tag along anytime." The look he sent her implied his invitation included more than work.

Emboldened, she asked, "What if I took you up on that offer?"

"Nothing would make me happier. You're a good assistant. And those spreadsheets you did for me, they're a whole lot better than what I came up with."

His praise sent a ribbon of warmth winding through her.

She inclined her head at Ace's mother and uncle. "Whatever they're talking about must be serious."

Ace looked over. "Numbers, I imagine," he said, finishing his sandwich.

"Numbers?"

"How many cows are pregnant, what's the anticipated herd size next year, how many calves to sell off, how many acres of alfalfa should we plant, what the current price of seed is. Want me to continue, or have I sufficiently bored you?"

Flynn whistled. "There's a lot to this ranching business." The only cattle her father had owned were a few calves for roping practice.

"Which is why we have to keep up our strength." Ace held out his brownie.

She caved. "All right, but just half."

He broke the brownie in two, giving her the larger portion.

They sat for a moment in silence, enjoying the sunshine and listening to the conversations around them.

"What do you like best about your job?" Flynn eventually asked.

"Not the paperwork, that's for sure."

"Me, either, though I'm actually pretty good at it."

"Not the headaches and the infinite little details that seem to pile up, either."

"Kind of like me and school."

Ace glanced around. "On the other hand, I love days like this, being outside with the animals. Solving problems, overcoming challenges. That's what keeps me interested."

"Challenges like Midnight?"

"When I figure out what makes that horse tick, I'm throwing a party." He took a sip of his soda. "What about you? What do you like best about your job?"

"Helping people," she answered without hesitation. "I don't have as much direct patient contact as the nurses and doctors, but when their experience is a little better, a little easier because of me, they're grateful. For the most part. It's what makes me want to go to work every day."

"We should all be so lucky to feel passionate about our jobs."

"It's the same for you. Like when you helped the Andersons with Lovey."

"I suppose."

She bumped elbows with him. "Stop being such a guy and admit it."

He laughed. "Okay, you got me. I like helping people. And animals. Even fluffy little kittens."

She lifted her gaze to him and said softly, "I bet you do like kittens."

"Babies, too."

Her heart flip-flopped.

This wasn't good. If she expected to protect herself from the temptations Ace Hart presented, she couldn't go all mushy inside just because he said "baby" in that silky voice of his.

She was strong, she could resist.

And she might have succeeded if he hadn't reached up and brushed a lock of flyaway hair from her face. The sensation of his fingers brushing her skin sent shivers coursing through her.

Steady, girl.

He leaned in, and her willpower flew out the window.

Kiss me.

Someone passed close to the truck, saving Flynn from making a fool of herself.

"Looks like lunch is over." She leaped to her feet.

People were up from their makeshift seats and starting back to work.

Ace didn't mention their close encounter, and neither did Flynn. For the next two hours they continued working in tandem, their established routine like a well-oiled machine.

Fortunately, Flynn barely had a spare second to recall their almost PDA. When she did, her pulse skipped erratically and her mind wandered.

"Flynn?"

"Sorry." Heat infused her cheeks. How long had Ace been talking to her before she heard him?

"We're done."

"We are?"

"That was the last calf for today. We'll finish with the strays tomorrow."

She glanced at the clipboard and then her watch. "It's only three o'clock."

"We've been at it since seven. Aren't you ready to call it a day?"

Not exactly. "Yeah, sure."

She helped him pack up and carry the supplies to his truck.

He closed the side compartment on his truck, stood, waited and finally said, "We could go out, if you want."

Alarm bells went off in her head. Hadn't she been avoiding him all week so as not to encourage him?

"Go where?" she asked.

A gleam lit his mesmerizing dark eyes. "Fishing."

Fishing! At Thunder Creek. Like they used to do when they were dating.

The alarm bells clanged louder.

"I don't know. I'm filthy." She plucked at the front of her shirt.

"We have time if you want to take a quick shower. The fish won't start biting till dusk."

Every logical and rational brain cell in her head screamed at her to tell him no. To go fishing with Ace was asking for trouble. Too many memories, good and bad.

She opened her mouth and what came out was: "Sure. Why not?"

Ace drove home after dropping Flynn off. They agreed he'd return for her in a half hour, which didn't give him much time.

The first thing he did when he walked into the kitchen was throw together some food to take, pilfering items from the refrigerator without much thought. The same with the pantry. Cheese, cold cuts, crackers, olives, strawberries, granola bars, anything that looked the least bit edible.

Okay, maybe not granola bars. Cookies instead. She'd liked the brownies at lunch. When he finished packing the food he grabbed some bottled water.

Kind of a mishmash dinner, but it would suffice.

Next he hit the bathroom where he washed up, then changed into a clean shirt and jeans. Last, he headed to the garage and retrieved the fishing gear. Good, he still had a few jars of bait and his lures weren't a tangled mess.

Before leaving he stopped quickly to check on Midnight. Fancy Gal, the stallion's constant companion, came over to the fence for a petting along with the other mares.

To Ace's amazement and delight, Midnight came, too. Willingly. Almost eagerly. Without Ace using a carrot to bribe him.

"Nothing like having the love of a good woman to make us complacent, is there, boy?"

Ace envied the horse. He wanted to know that same feeling with Flynn.

It could happen. She'd agreed to go fishing.

She wasn't waiting for him when he pulled

up in front of the house. Instead, Earl stood at the top of the porch steps, rocking on his heels and wearing an unreadable expression. Ace hadn't seen or spoken to Flynn's father since the Western Frontier Pro Rodeo when Fancy Gal had colic. When Earl had seen Ace and Flynn kissing.

She'd mentioned once that Earl was happy about the baby. He might be less happy that Ace was the father.

He got out of the truck, his nerves on edge. Despite being almost thirty, Flynn was still her father's little girl and the love of his life.

"Howdy, Earl."

"Ace. Good to see you. Flynn will be right out."

They met at the foot of the porch steps and shook hands. Ace breathed a sigh of relief. "How've you been?"

If he thought to engage Earl in small talk, he was very wrong.

"You be careful with my Flynn."

"I will. I'll watch her every step, make sure she doesn't slip and fall."

"I'm not talking about the creek."

Of course not. "I won't hurt her. You can count on it."

"You did before."

"She told you?"

"She didn't have to."

Ace wouldn't make the mistake of under-estimating Earl again.

His attention was distracted by the appear-ance of three individuals from around the corner of the house. From their dress and manner, he identified them as a real estate agent and her clients.

The woman gave Ace a polite smile, then spoke to Earl. "Thank you for letting us see the place on such short notice."

"No problem."

"We'll be in touch."

They would be in touch. If the clients' ex-cited glow was any indication, they liked what they saw.

Ace was glad for Earl. Not so glad for him-self.

He waited by the porch swing, just beyond hearing distance, trying not to think about Flynn moving and failing miserably. After a round of handshakes, the real estate agent and her clients left.

Earl's smile was much too tickled pink for Ace's liking.

"That went well," Ace said, rejoining Earl.

His reply was a satisfied grunt, not that Ace expected details.

Thirty to sixty days for an escrow to close. He couldn't afford to waste one second.

Flynn stepped through the front door. "Sorry I'm late." Her glance traveled from her father to Ace. "Everything okay?"

"They seemed taken with the place." Earl went to her and kissed her cheek. "And they're already prequalified for a home loan."

"Did they make an offer?"

"The Realtor said she'd be calling later today and then she winked at me."

It was even worse than Ace first thought.

"Dad, that's great!"

Earl grunted again, with even more satisfaction. "Don't be late, you two. That road isn't easy to drive in the dark."

Ace couldn't talk, his throat had gone dry.

He helped Flynn into the truck. She'd changed her clothes and carried a canvas tote which he stowed behind the seat.

"I brought some snacks along," she said when they were underway.

"Me, too," he mumbled.

"Then I guess we won't starve."

He tried to laugh but couldn't muster more

than a weak chuckle. "Your dad was pretty happy."

"About what?"

"The ranch selling."

"I'm not going to celebrate until everyone's signed on the dotted line."

Maybe not, but her eyes glinted with undeniable optimism.

A stilted silence descended on them for the remainder of the drive.

Ace mentally kicked himself for not kissing her at lunch. No way in hell would he let a second opportunity pass without taking advantage of it.

At the creek, they unloaded the food and fishing gear. Ace insisted on carrying everything except the tackle box and blanket. Even then, he held Flynn's arm as they descended the slope to the bank.

She stayed behind and laid out the blanket on the only relatively flat spot in the area while he made two more trips back and forth to the truck.

She was stripping off her shirt when he returned with the lawn chairs. Beneath the shirt, she wore a bikini top.

Ace froze. "What's going on?" he croaked.

She bent and rolled up the legs of her

denim Capri pants. "It's so warm out, I thought I'd get a little sun while we fished."

Fished? He blinked. For a moment, he'd forgotten where they were and what they were doing.

She promptly reminded him. "Come on, slowpoke."

It wasn't the sight of her skimpy top that immobilized him, but the gentle curve of her belly poking out above the waistband of her pants.

Flynn was noticeably pregnant and she'd never looked sexier.

Chapter 13

Fishing pole in HAND, Flynn stepped gingerly off the bank and into the brisk water. Her toes curled inside her sneakers, which sank into the soft creek bed.

"Where you going?" Ace asked, his voice unsteady.

Was it the creek or Flynn unbalancing him?

"The pool."

Unless flooding this past spring had drastically altered the topography of the creek bank, there was a large pool just around the bend and several boulders providing perfect seating.

"Wait for me."

Ace's gaze on her bare back sent a series of tiny tremors racing along her spine.

She waded deeper into the creek, using the cool water to extinguish her burning thoughts.

He'd seen her in a bathing suit before. Countless times. Seen her entirely naked more than once. Here, in fact, when they'd gone skinny-dipping. Why today did the sight of a little skin cause him to stare at her with hungry eyes?

Flynn wasn't the siren type. She didn't attempt to charm men with her feminine wiles. She might have given it a try if they panted after her like Ace was apparently doing.

It was so unlike him, so unlike her, she almost burst into laughter.

"Don't dawdle." She glanced behind her, and the laugh she'd been holding back died.

Ace had removed his shirt, too.

His muscled chest and arms gleamed in the bright sunlight, as did his dark brown hair. The contrast was quite…appealing.

A memory surfaced, almost painful in its intensity. She'd run her hands along those same muscles, felt them bunch beneath her fingertips as he'd hovered over her, nibbled her neck, slid a knee between her legs to part them.

Her sneaker abruptly slipped on a moss-covered rock, and she teetered for a moment before regaining her balance.

"Be careful," he warned. "The current's pretty strong."

He entered the creek, creating a small splash. Along with his fishing pole, he carried the tackle box.

She eyed it pointedly. "You think I'm going to lose my hook?"

"It's happened before." Ace had nearly drowned once trying to unsnag her hook that had become caught in an underwater trap. "Today I'm cutting the line."

This was much better, thought Flynn. She hadn't liked the somber mood on the drive over.

He was going to have to get used to the idea of her father selling the ranch. Possibly soon if the potential buyers today made an offer.

She was going to have to get used to the idea, too.

A month ago she wouldn't have been torn. She'd have left Roundup without a second's hesitation.

Since then, her relationship with Ace had changed. The question was, into what?

She loved him. The miserable, hopeless kind of love. Not head over heels. That had been back in college, before Ace broke her heart. He wasn't now and never had been anywhere approaching the edge of that mysterious and magical realm she resided in, much less crossed over into it.

And she was tired of being stuck in there alone.

Appreciative glances and tiny tremors were all well and good, but Flynn wanted spontaneous declarations, can't-wait-until-he-calls flutters and secretive glances across the dinner table that no one else understood.

She wanted him to love her. Love her beyond reason.

The farther along the creek they traveled, the faster the water rushed by them. Flynn shivered as it swirled past her knees.

"Cold?"

"No." She turned, her eyes instantly drawn to Ace's wet jeans clinging to his thighs. "Maybe a little."

What a lie! Chilled was the last thing she felt.

"We can go back," he said.

"Wimp," she teased, hoping to distract herself as much as him. "The bend is right there."

"You sure you're okay?"

"I'm fine."

"I promised your dad I'd watch out for you."

The genuine anxiety in his voice caused her to look at herself through his eyes, a pregnant woman traipsing along a creek. She conceded his concern wasn't overblown.

She also conceded she might be trying to prove something—to Ace and herself. Exert her independence.

Suddenly, her interest in fishing diminished.

Not enough for her to suggest returning, however.

The creek abruptly widened, the water becoming warmer and more sluggish as they entered the pool.

"If there are any fish in here," Ace commented, "we've scared them away."

"They'll come back."

The boulders were where they'd always been since Flynn and Ace started coming here, jutting up from the ground like giant mushrooms. She parked herself on the first one, pulling her sodden sneakers out of the water.

Ace sat down so quickly, he wobbled. "Whoa!"

"You'd think a man as good as you are at riding broncs could sit a boulder."

"Different skill set required." He set the tackle box down on a wide, flat rock. "Need me to bait your hook?"

"Sir, you insult me." Truthfully, Flynn had always been the better and more avid fisherman.

Soon their bobbers were dancing merrily on the water's glittering surface and conversation flowed easily.

"Did you see today when that mama cow butted Harlan right in the…" Flynn cut her gaze to her lap. "I never heard a grown man yelp so loud."

"Or so high," Ace added with a grin.

"And your poor cousin Beau. I swear, he stepped in every cow patty there was."

"It was like his boots had built-in homing devices."

They shared a few more chuckles. After a while, the sun's soothing rays gave Flynn a case of the lazies.

"I guess the fish aren't biting today," Ace murmured.

"There's no rush."

Sometimes doing nothing together could be just as enjoyable as doing something.

"Tell me a secret." She flashed him a mischievous grin.

"Forget it."

"Come on. I'll go first."

It was a game they'd played in their dating days. Sharing secrets. Mostly funny ones. Occasionally sad. Now and then a little shocking.

As far as Flynn knew, neither of them had revealed their secrets to a single soul.

They'd trusted each other in those days.

She needed to trust him again.

Without waiting for him to answer, she blurted, "I cheated on an advanced calculus midterm. Bought the answers from some kid."

Ace's jaw went slack. "You're kidding!"

"I was sick the week before the test. Bronchitis. I studied. Tried to. My brain was mush. Math was always hard for me. I couldn't afford less than a C in the class."

"Miss Goody Two-shoes Flynn cheated on a test." He shook his head in dismay, but one corner of his mouth tilted in a grin.

"Only that one time. I was desperate. I worked my tail off the rest of the semester to make up for it."

After a moment, Ace admitted, "I got drunk after my dad's funeral."

"Sorry, Ace, but that's no secret. We could tell."

"I was drunk for two straight days."

She sat back. "Really?"

"And hungover for four."

"Ow!"

"The worst part is, I repeated it after you and I broke up."

Now, that *was* a secret.

"I still thought about you every day," she confessed. *And every night.* "Even when I was married."

"I've only dated three women since you."

"That's no secret, either." She swung her fishing pole back and forth, watching the line slice through the water. "Dinah told me."

"They all dumped me. For the same reason."

"Which was?"

"I think the exact quote went, 'I'm tired of being with a guy who's hung up on his old girlfriend.'"

Flynn's hand froze. "Is it true?"

"You know it is."

That was the problem, she knew no such thing. "Why did you leave me that morning?"

He stared at the distant mountains, his reply, if he was even going to give her one, trapped in his throat.

Don't shut me out now. Not like before.

"The simple answer is I got scared." He spoke slowly. Reservedly. "The complicated answer is…more complicated."

"Let's stick to simple, then," she gently urged. "Scared of what?"

He turned his head to look at her. "You."

"What did I do that was scary?" Flynn hadn't been clingy or needy or demanding. Not anything that typically scared off men. Now or then.

"You took my breath away."

"I don't understand."

"That's the complicated part. Us, being together, it was unexpected. I wasn't ready."

"For what?"

"The feelings I had for you. *Have* for you. It's different this time."

Flynn noticed she was gripping the fishing pole like a lifeline and relaxed her grip. "Different how?"

"Stronger."

"Doesn't sound like a reason to rush off. Sounds more like a reason to stay."

"The timing sucked. My mom and I were signing the loan documents that morning, finalizing our expansion plans. I'd just taken on another new client the Andersons recommended. We were entering contract negotiations with two new rodeo promoters. It wasn't fair to start something I couldn't finish."

"You seriously thought rushing off and not so much as sending me a one-line text wouldn't hurt?" Flynn's eyes stung with unshed tears. She blinked them away before Ace saw.

"Not as much."

"As what? Dating for a few weeks and then dumping me?" She reeled in her line.

"Yes."

"Because you did it before?"

"Breaking up with you was one of the hardest things I've ever done."

"Hmm. So, by leaving that morning you were sparing yourself difficulty. Not me."

"You're twisting this around." He reeled in his line, too. Yanked it in was a better description.

"I think I'm calling it exactly right."

Fishing, playing secrets, both had been bad

ideas. She slid off the boulder and into the creek, the cool water giving her a jolt.

"Flynn, wait."

"What are we doing? What's changed that you're suddenly not too busy to have me in your life? Ah, yes, the baby." She cut him off before he could answer. "You have time for him or her but not me."

Pole in hand, she trudged forward, the current impeding her progress.

"Don't go," he said.

"Why is it okay for you to always take off and not me?"

He came after her, water sloshing, tackle box swinging. "I was wrong."

"Which time?"

"I should have called you. Explained."

"News flash, Ace." Anger propelled her forward. "That would have made it only infinitesimally better."

They reached the bank where they'd left the blanket and their gear. The slope looked higher than Flynn remembered, and she hesitated.

"Let me go first."

"I can do it." She raised a foot, teetered unsteadily.

Ace grabbed her by the arm. "Quit being so stubborn."

"Fine." She moved to the side and watched as he effortlessly scaled the bank. "Show off," she grumbled under her breath.

Situated on solid ground, he reached out a hand to her.

She accepted it grudgingly. The next second, she was hoisted onto the bank. Ace circled her waist with one strong arm, though it was completely unnecessary.

"You can let go."

He didn't and instead increased his hold on her.

"Ace—"

"Here's another secret." He lowered his head and brushed his lips across hers. "I left that morning because I realized how easy it would be to fall for you. That I probably already had years ago and kept denying it."

Quite a line for a man who typically held his cards close to his chest.

Flynn's resolve melted. He may not love her to distraction, but he obviously had genuine feelings for her. Or, perhaps he did love her and simply refused to admit it.

Either way, he was making it hard to resist him.

He pressed his hand to her belly, splayed his fingers wide. "We're going to be a family. Nothing or no one will come between me and you and our child."

In that moment, Flynn let herself believe him. He was here, with her, taking time away from work. Fishing, of all things, because that was what she'd wanted.

He kissed her then, vanquishing all coherent thoughts and leaving only sensation. A thrumming pulse. A quickening in her middle. Tingling nerve endings.

She ceased fighting it and gave in to her body's electric response.

Before Flynn quite realized what was happening, Ace swooped her up in his arms and carried her to the blanket. Setting her on her feet, he resumed kissing her, his tongue demanding and receiving an eager and willing response from her.

It had been like this before when they made love. She'd lost her head, surrendered to the wildly sensual feelings he aroused in her with just a kiss. A caress. A murmured word. A low groan.

She'd made a mistake.

Not the baby. Heavens, no. That was wonderful. Incredible. But the hurt in the wake of his leaving… She couldn't cope a third time.

Despite his recent efforts, nothing about his work and commitments had changed. Ace's ability to devote himself to her depended entirely on his job demands, which were numerous.

He must have sensed her reservations, for he tore his mouth away from hers and gazed intently at her. "We don't have to do this if you're not ready."

Seemed kind of silly for her to refuse him when she was carrying his child.

"I'm not going to run out on you afterward," he said, a rough edge to his voice. "I swear."

She didn't think he would. Not today. Not if he wanted to see her again before the baby was born.

Nonetheless, doubts lingered.

"I slept with you before because I thought there was a chance for us," she said. "A possible future."

"There is. More than ever."

"You left me. Twice. It isn't easy for me to lay open my heart to you a third time."

"I want to marry you, Flynn. Be the kind of husband you deserve."

Do you love me? She almost blurted the question out loud.

What would his response be if she did?

"I'm afraid."

"Of what?" He stroked her cheek with the pad of his thumb.

They had stood there before, in the same spot, Ace kissing her senseless. He was very hard to resist, and Flynn was no longer sure she wanted to.

"This, us…matters to me," she said.

"Me, too."

"I wouldn't be here with you, wouldn't have invited you into my bed, if I didn't care greatly for you."

It was the closest she'd come to admitting she loved him.

He gathered her into his arms. "I won't hurt you."

"You can't make that promise. Who knows what will happen?"

"I won't hurt you intentionally."

People seldom did. Tell *that* to the pain when she was curled on her bed, crying herself sick.

Here was Flynn's chance to say no. To tell Ace his track record stank and she refused to set herself up for another big disappointment.

But then he pressed those incredible hands into the small of her bare back, and what came out of her mouth was a tiny moan of acquiescence.

Ace gently lowered her onto the blanket. She barely noticed the rough ground beneath them, her attention was focused entirely on them. His smoldering dark eyes, the sharp inhalation of her breath, the small currents of desire zinging through them both as he struggled to restrain his need.

They'd never come together when he didn't thrill her, and today was no exception.

He settled beside her, his hand roaming her body. Every now and then he paused to explore further, trace the slope of her waist, the curve of her hip. She arched, sighed, quaked when his fingers strayed to a particularly sensitive spot.

Sliding on top of her, he kissed her mouth, her neck, the soft mounds of her breasts spilling out of her bikini top. Inch by tantalizing inch, he worked his way down to her rounded tummy.

With one swift jerk, he unfastened the top of her pants, exposing more skin and the edge of her sheer panties.

"You are so beautiful," he whispered, his breath warm against her skin. "So perfect."

She wriggled when he kissed her navel,

then writhed when he traced the outline with his tongue.

Abruptly, he moved up her body, his lips stopping every few seconds for a taste of her. Reaching her bikini top, he tugged the flimsy fabric aside, then closed his mouth around her nipple.

Pregnancy had made Flynn's breasts more sensitive. She raised off the blanket as fire shot through her. Ace helped her out of her bathing suit top, not waiting for her to lie back down before covering her breasts with his hands. She pulled his head down, silently urging him to take her in his mouth again.

He didn't stop there. Sliding his hand into the opening of her jeans, he breached her panties and found her damp center. She shifted her hips in response, willing him to soothe the burning ache inside her.

Thankfully, Ace had always been attuned to her during their lovemaking and very accommodating.

When she could stand no more, when her need demanded satisfaction, she rolled him over onto his back and straddled his middle.

"Hey, what's this?" he asked, his initial shock quickly replaced by a wicked grin.

"Why should you get all the fun?"

She ran her open palms over the muscled planes of his chest, combed her fingers through the patch of crinkly chest hair, stroked the smooth expanse of his taut stomach.

Talk about perfection.

He reached for her breasts, but she caught his hands and returned them to his sides.

"Not yet."

He groaned with frustration.

She squirmed down his body, eliciting more groans, until she reached his thighs. Once there, she unsnapped his jeans, exposing him as he had her.

He was ready for her, his arousal unmistakable.

She teased him through the fabric of his briefs, and he ground out her name on a ragged breath. Just as her fingers closed around him, he grasped her shoulders and pulled her down on top of him. The next second, he rolled them over so that they faced each other.

Smiling seductively, she slid her jeans off.

Ace pinned her beneath him and entered her. Slowly. Deeply. Flynn cried out from the pure joy of it. Each thrust took her to a new place, a new level of awareness.

Soon, however, she craved more.

Curling her arms around his neck, she brought his ear to her mouth.

"Harder," she whispered. "Faster."

"I don't want to hurt the baby."

"You won't."

"Sweetheart, I—"

She lifted her hips to meet his. "You *won't*."

Still, he held back, until Flynn reached a hand between their joined bodies. Then he lost control, which had been her plan all along.

Her climax hit her with sudden and exquisite force, leaving her shaken and weak and utterly sated. Ace cupped her face between his hands. When she would have closed her eyes, he demanded, "Look at me."

She complied. With their gazes locked and her mind crying out her love for him, his body shuddered in release. Flynn held him, willing the moment to last and last.

Stroking his back, she clung to him, the setting sun warming them with the last of its rays. Soon, before she was quite ready, he rolled off and snuggled her close.

He brushed at her hair. Flynn hated to think what it looked like and laughed with embarrassment.

"I like it when you do that," he said, and nuzzled her ear.

"Laugh?"

"Yeah, your eyes light up."

She tried to hide her face in his neck. He wouldn't let her and continued to stare at her with such unabashed emotion, she forgot about her embarrassment.

"That was wonderful." She skimmed her finger along the stubble on his jaw.

"Marry me, Flynn."

Like that, her complacent mood evaporated.

"We can be good parents to our child without a marriage license hanging on the wall."

"I don't want you to move."

"That's not a good enough reason." She sat up, silently scolding herself for not anticipating this. "It's no reason at all."

"You owe it to our child to give us a chance."

She saw in his eyes her refusal had struck a nerve.

Rising to her feet, she tugged on her clothes. If he'd told her he loved her and then proposed, her reaction would be entirely different.

"We've been through this before."

He also stood and dressed. "Just because

your mother walked out on you and your family doesn't mean the same thing will happen to us."

This time he'd struck a nerve with her.

Why did he have to go and ruin everything by proposing and then bringing up her mother?

"I don't think we should date anymore."

"Come on, Flynn."

"It feels like you're trying to ease your guilty conscience. Not…"

"Not what?"

"Nothing."

If he couldn't proclaim his love for her after what they'd just shared, she was wasting her time.

"What do I have to do to prove myself?"

"I don't know." She started shoving items in her tote bag.

"There has to be something."

She said the first idiotic thing that popped into her head. "Call me a hundred times between tonight and tomorrow."

"That's all?"

"It's a safe bet. You won't have the time."

"Tell you what." He thrust his arms into his shirtsleeves. "I call you a hundred times by eight o'clock tomorrow morning, you agree to spend the entire weekend with me, from Friday night to Sunday evening."

"I'm scheduled for a half shift on Saturday."

"Then, any time you're not at the clinic."

"But you have to work."

"Maybe I won't."

"This I have to see." Flynn was confident she'd be spending the weekend alone.

She reached for a corner of the blanket, intending to fold it. Suddenly, a muffled trilling came from inside the tote bag. Her cell phone.

She dug it out, checked the display and gaped at Ace, who held his cell phone to his ear.

"You've got to be kidding." She hit the End button, rejecting the call.

He grinned. "One down, ninety-nine to go."

Chapter 14

There were days when Flynn felt like a child on a sugar high and could barely sit still. Others, her eyelids drooped and her feet dragged and she stared greedily at people drinking caffeine-infused beverages like a dog waiting for a treat.

Fortunately, today was the sugar-high kind of day. If not, she wouldn't be able to handle her and Ace's upcoming hike along Bent Arrow Bute.

She'd actually wanted to go horseback riding, her favorite pastime for beautiful Saturday mornings. Ace naturally nixed the idea, and they'd compromised on hiking.

He'd loaded their backpacks. His was the heavier one and contained most of their supplies, which, for a day hike, weren't many. Judging by the weight of her backpack, she was carrying a bag of roasted almonds and a travel-size package of wet wipes.

The trail Ace had chosen was for novices. Another compromise. Flynn told herself not to argue. It was important to him that he do things for her, watch over her, even though she felt completely capable. What really mattered was they were spending the entire weekend together. No interruptions except for her half shift at the clinic this afternoon.

He'd won the bet, called her a hundred times before eight in the morning. She'd shut her phone off at ten and woke up eight hours later to fifty-seven missed calls. Had he slept at all?

As a result, they were hiking this morning and having dinner this evening. Pizza and wings. She'd caved. Tomorrow they were watching NASCAR races on television and grilling burgers.

Flynn smiled to herself. She'd won the bet, too.

They were nearing the trailhead where

their hike would commence when Ace's cell phone rang.

"Hey, Uncle Josh. What's up?" His expression changed from happy-go-lucky to concerned. "Where are you?" After a brief exchange of information, Ace pulled over and put the truck in park. "Send Beau and the rig with the bulls ahead. I'll make some calls. See what I can line up. I'll get back to you shortly."

"What's wrong?" Flynn asked when he'd disconnected.

"One of the trucks broke down on the way to an amateur rodeo in Bozeman. Uncle Josh thinks the alternator has gone bad. They're stuck on the side of the highway about twenty-five miles outside of Roundup."

"Oh, no!"

"Uncle Josh called for roadside assistance. The service station is backed up and can't guarantee a repair truck there for at least three or four hours."

"Why so long?"

"They didn't say."

"Will your uncle make the rodeo in time?"

"That's the problem. I'm going to see who's available to meet with them and swap out trucks. That way, Uncle Josh and Colt can get back on the road. Whoever I get a hold of can wait for the repair truck."

Flynn listened as Ace placed call after call to various ranch hands. Everyone was either unable to break away, out riding the range, not answering his call for whatever reason or, like Colt, on route to the rodeo with their uncle Joshua.

Swearing ripely, Ace tossed his cell phone onto the seat.

Flynn sensed his next remark and braced herself for a rush of disappointment.

"I'm sorry." His tone was contrite. "I'm going to have to rescue them. If I leave now, I can be there in an hour. Less if I drive fast."

"Isn't there someone else you can call? What about your cousins?"

"Duke's on duty today and Beau is with Uncle Josh."

"No other employees?"

"It's the weekend. A lot of them are off."

"Would they be willing to work this once?"

"It's not right for me to ask them just so I can take the day off."

"Why not? You put in more hours than they do."

"It's my ranch, my responsibility, not theirs."

"You deserve a day off, too."

"Not if it endangers our livestock. Those horses can't wait on the side of the road long and be in any shape for the rodeo. It's a one-night event. Tonight. No time for them to recuperate if they're stressed."

Flynn sighed, annoyed at herself as much as anything. "I understand. I'm not intentionally being petty."

"And I know you're disappointed."

Better than half of the dates they went on were cut short or interrupted by some emergency call.

"You can come with me," he suggested, raising his eyebrows.

"I have to be at the clinic by two. That's cutting it kind of close."

"Can you trade shifts with someone?"

"I doubt I'd find someone this late."

There were some women who'd leap at the chance to be stuck in a vehicle with a handsome, sexy cowboy for hours on end.

Not Flynn. It wasn't that their hiking excursion had been canceled or that she'd miss her shift at the clinic. Rather, it was that Ace had gotten to the point where he assumed she'd go with him and relieve him from the difficult position of having to choose between her and work.

She was feeling taken for granted.

Not unlike when she'd been married.

Of course, someone had to help Ace's uncle. Those poor horses couldn't remain in that trailer. And the Harts had a contract with the rodeo promoter that needed to be fulfilled.

But couldn't Ace at least contact one or two of those men off work and ask if they'd be willing to drive the truck?

"It's okay, just take me home," she said.

He stroked her arm. "I'll make it up to you at dinner tonight."

"Call first. I'm sort of tired."

"Hey, now, a bet's a bet," he added with a mischievous grin.

"Yeah, it is," she answered pointedly.

"Flynn, I don't—"

"It's all right. Really."

Ace started the truck, his jaw muscles clenched tightly. He thought she was being churlish, she could tell.

She considered changing her mind. He couldn't help that the alternator on his uncle's truck went bad.

If only he'd tried a little bit harder to keep his promise, she might feel differently, might have gone with him.

She still could.

"This isn't by choice, you know."

"Enough with the apologizing," she bit out more sharply than necessary, and immediately regretted her outburst. "Work comes first."

And it would be the same after the baby was born.

Flynn watched the passing landscape. Maybe she shouldn't be so hard on Ace. In truth, if it had been a veterinary emergency interrupting their date, she probably would have gone with him and not minded at all.

What did that say about her?

"Let's skip grilling hamburgers tomorrow and drive into Billings for dinner. Dress up and go some place fancy."

He was trying to make amends. She should let him.

Except part of her wondered if this was how it would always be. Him having an emergency, her feeling hurt and disappointed. Him apologizing and scrambling to appease her.

The pattern was a familiar one, too similar to what she went through with Paul.

What if, like her ex-husband had done, Ace stopped trying after a while?

Not going to happen, not if Flynn could help it. They had a child to consider, a child she was determined would be first on both of their priority lists. To insure that, she'd have to put forth as much effort as Ace.

"Sure, we can go out to dinner tomorrow. That'll be nice."

He smiled, visibly relaxed. "Good."

"On one condition."

"Not another hundred phone calls."

"You don't cancel. For any reason. If something comes up, I don't care what it is, you'll either have to be creative, more determined than you were today or have a contingency plan in place."

"You're serious."

She shrugged. "If you're not up to the challenge…"

"I'm up to it," he scoffed. "Rest assured."

When Flynn walked in the kitchen door a short time later, her father was talking on the phone. He sent her a what-are-you-doing-home look.

"Long story," she mouthed, and headed to her bedroom where she changed out of her too-tight hiking shorts and into the roomiest pajama pants she could find. Pretty quick, she'd have to go shopping for maternity clothes. The prospect raised her spirits.

A knock sounded on her door. "You decent?"

"Come on in, Dad."

He wore an enormous grin.

"Did that couple finally make an offer?" She grabbed a ball cap off the bookcase and plunked it on her head, pulling her hair through the hole in the back.

"No, the real estate agent called yesterday, said they weren't interested unless I dropped the price some more. A lot more."

"Then why are you smiling?"

"That was the asset manager from the Missoula Cattle Company."

Her interest piqued. "The same company leasing the Harts' land?"

"Yep. They want to lease my land, too."

"All six hundred acres?"

"Except for the house. They said I can keep it and the barns and a few acres. They'll even pay for new fences."

She stared at him, his words yet to fully register. "We're not moving?"

"I am. You can stay here if you change your mind about school. Or, come with me. In that case, I'll probably rent the house out.

With the money the Missoula Cattle Company is willing to pay for leasing rights, I don't have to worry about selling."

"How long is the lease for?"

"Three years, with an option for three more." He practically danced with excitement. "It's an incredible deal."

"When do they want to take over?"

"Soon as I meet with them and sign the contract. This coming week. Though I was thinking I should probably have an attorney review the contract first. Just to be on the safe side."

"Good idea." Flynn sat on the bed, her legs suddenly unable to support her.

The day had arrived. They were leaving Roundup!

Or, she could stay here in the house. Close to Ace.

Choices. Options. She was once again faced with them and not a lot of time to decide.

"I'm going to call your sister."

"Sure," Flynn muttered at her father's retreating back.

After several moments of staring into space, she popped off the bed, went to her desk and fired up her laptop computer, logging on to the internet.

She decided to take the same advice she'd given Ace and promptly set about developing her own contingency plan, starting with a job search.

"Yeah, I see you." Ace squinted through the windshield at a tiny white truck and trailer about a half mile up the road. "Be there in a second."

He hung up with Colt, wondering how long this ordeal would last and wishing like heck Flynn had come with him. Why had she said no?

During the first half hour of his lonely drive, he decided she was angry that yet another of their dates was interrupted. During the second half of the drive, he considered the situation from her point of view.

Had he really tried as hard as he could to get someone else to rescue the stranded truck?

The more he thought about it, the more he realized the answer was no. Had Flynn not been with him, he would have gotten on the road immediately. Attempting to find someone else, making calls, had been strictly for her benefit.

What he'd wanted was for her to go with him like before.

That she hadn't readily agreed confused him. Frustrated him. Irritated him.

Like before.

His own words hit home.

Why should she be the one to always compromise?

Regardless of what happened, he couldn't let anything go wrong at dinner tomorrow night. Flynn was right about another thing. He needed a contingency plan. Someone he could count on in a pinch.

As he pulled up behind the stranded truck and trailer, Colt stepped into view and greeted him with a wave.

No reason his brother shouldn't help him.

Unhooking a trailer filled with horses wasn't an easy feat. The livestock had to be unloaded in order to lighten the trailer. Vehicles slowed as they passed the orange safety cones Uncle Joshua set out, their occupants gawking at the sight of ten horses tied to the outside of a trailer.

Ace was grateful the rig hauling the bulls hadn't been the one to break down. Then they might have surely caused an accident.

Once the trailer was unhooked, they were faced with the task of rolling the nonrunning truck ahead and out of the way. Between the two of them, Ace and Colt were able to push the truck while Uncle Joshua steered. They all three were sweating profusely by the time they'd hooked the trailer up to Ace's truck and finished reloading the last horse.

Colt slipped in behind the wheel, Uncle Joshua in the passenger seat. All things considered, it could have gone much worse.

Ace called the service station and received an update on their estimated arrival.

Colt rolled down his window. "How long?"

"Two to three hours," Ace grumbled.

That was the problem with living in a small town and no sizable metropolis nearby. Few resources. Fortunately, he'd brought a few files along and could tackle some work while he waited.

He stepped up to the driver's side window. "Before you leave, I have a favor to ask."

"What's up?" Colt accepted the cold soda Uncle Joshua procured from their travel ice chest. "We really need to get on the road if we're going to make it before the rodeo starts."

"I'm taking Flynn into Billings for a special dinner tomorrow night. Someplace nice."

Colt flashed Ace his trademark jaunty grin. "If you're looking for the name of a good restaurant—"

"I can manage the date. What I need is for you to stick nearby and cover for me in case something comes up."

"Can't. Already made plans. I'll be out of town."

"You're leaving on a Sunday afternoon?"

"Something came up. I'll be back Tuesday."

"Two days? Why didn't you tell me?"

"I didn't know for sure I was going until an hour ago. I was waiting on a phone call. Can't you change your date with Flynn?"

"I already promised her." And Ace refused to ask Flynn to move their dinner to Tuesday. Not for an excuse as flimsy as Colt received some phone call and was disappearing for two days.

"Where are you going?"

"I have business."

"What kind of business?"

"Personal," he said, his voice low and terse.

Colt had been acting stranger and stranger in recent weeks, and Ace was getting tired of it.

"This leaving all the time has to stop."

"You're not my keeper."

"And you're not just an employee. You're a member of the family. We all depend on the livestock contracting business to support us. You can't continue taking off whenever the mood strikes."

"You're taking off tomorrow night."

"Sunday. Not Monday. You have an obligation, a responsibility."

Colt's features shut down. "Don't lecture me."

"Someone needs to."

"I'm not staying home just to babysit while you go on a date."

Ace's anger erupted. "Why the hell not? I stay home every time you take off for some rodeo."

"This is important."

"So's my dinner with Flynn. We're having a baby."

An odd emotion flickered across Colt's face, and he shoved the transmission into drive. "Uncle Joshua can help you."

Up until then, their uncle had remained out of the conversation. "Whatever you need, Ace."

Colt eased the truck and trailer slowly forward, effectively putting an end to the conversation.

"We're talking when you get home," Ace hollered after them, doubting Colt heard.

Where was a punching bag when you needed one?

Between Flynn, the truck breaking down and his disagreement with his brother, Ace was feeling perfectly dandy.

Three hours sitting on the side of the road in a truck with no air-conditioning and nothing but a few work files and his own thoughts for company didn't improve matters. Neither did the mechanic, who took almost an hour to complete a simple repair. Ace practically had steam pouring out of his ears when the man finally finished.

Nothing sounded better than the truck's engine roaring to life.

"This here replacement battery will get you home but not much further," the mechanic advised. "You're going to need to bring the truck in for a new alternator."

"Appreciate the help." Ace presented his credit card for the total of the bill.

"Sorry it took so long. We're short one man today."

Ace knew the feeling.

His tension ebbed only slightly as he drove home, his truck eating up the miles. He checked the dash clock. Barring any unforeseen complications, he'd reach Thunder Ranch by four. He could throw on some fresh clothes, see to a few chores and be at Flynn's by six.

Not too late for supper and a stroll around the center of town.

She'd told him to call first.

He grabbed his phone off the seat, only to have it ring in his hand. A number he didn't recognize appeared on the display.

Ace didn't answer. If the call was important, the person would leave a message. They didn't.

Good. Turns out practicing restraint wasn't that tough.

He changed his mind about calling Flynn, not taking a chance she'd say no, and decided instead to simply show up. Even if he only got to stay a few minutes, he'd let her know she was the one person he wanted to see most at the end of a long and arduous day.

Anticipation had him putting pedal to the metal.

His mother knocked on his bedroom door as he was changing. "There's some leftover pot roast I can heat up if you're hungry."

He opened the door, tucking in his shirt. "Maybe later. I'm heading over to Flynn's. I won't be late."

"All right."

"You feeling okay, Mom? You look beat." It seemed he was asking her that same question a lot lately.

"I spent most of the day on the monthly financials. Not my strong suit, and it wore me out." She rubbed her chest beneath her collarbone.

"Mine, either, or I'd help you."

"You do enough already."

"So do you. How are the financials looking, by the way?"

She shrugged. "We're getting by."

"It'd be better if we had those stud fees coming in."

"Have you tried another hand breeding?"

"Later this week. I'm waiting for a mare to come into heat."

"I'm sure it'll go well. Midnight's making great progress." She stood on tiptoes and kissed Ace's cheek. "Tell Flynn hello for me and invite her over. I'd love to see her."

"There was a young couple looking at her dad's place the other day. They seemed pretty interested."

"Then you'd better hurry and win her over."

He thought of dinner tomorrow. "I'm working on it. Trust me."

Ace parked behind Flynn's house and

jogged to the kitchen door, knocking briskly. She must have been standing right there, for a second later she tugged the tiny curtain aside and peeked out at him.

The door promptly swung wide. "Hey."

"I know I should have called first."

"Come on in." She stepped back. "I'm assuming the vehicle swapping went okay."

"More or less. I have to drop the truck off at the shop on Monday for a new alternator."

He gave her a hug, noticing she wore an oversize T-shirt and leggings. Definitely lounge wear and not strolling-around-the-center-of-town wear. The faint sounds of canned laughter floated in from the family room.

"You watching TV?"

"Actually, I've been in my room on the computer. Just came out to the kitchen to start dinner when I heard you knock." As if suddenly reminded, she went to a simmering pot on the stove and stirred the contents.

"I wasn't planning on staying." Ace's hope for an evening together were dashed when she said nothing about joining her and her father. "Just came by to say hi and make sure you were all right." Make sure *they* were all right. "And to apologize for earlier."

"Again?" She crossed her arms over her waist, which emphasized the small mound of her belly. "This is becoming a habit."

She wasn't entirely kidding, he could tell.

Did he apologize to her that much?

Did he screw up that much?

"You were right, I should have tried to reach a few more people today before giving up. I have this tendency to think I'm the only one who can resolve a problem."

"You don't say?"

Her sparkling smile encouraged him. He covered the distance separating them in two strides.

"I missed you."

Without giving her a chance to respond, he took her in his arms, covered her mouth with his and proceeded to show her just how big a fool he'd been.

She returned his kiss with a burst of passion that surprised him as much as it excited him. If not for her father in the family room, Ace would have swept her into his arms and stolen her away to her bedroom.

Instead, he released her. Reluctantly. Waited for his pounding heart to slow. "Maybe I should stay."

She smiled coyly, letting Ace know how much she liked unbalancing him.

He stumbled to the kitchen table and dropped into a chair. A half-dozen papers were fanned out in front of him. The headings jumped off the pages, striking him like tiny darts.

Employment Application.

He picked up the closest one. It was for a hospital in Billings. His heart resumed pounding, but for a different reason. "What's this?"

Flynn glanced over from the stove, let out a small sigh. "I was going to tell you tomorrow at dinner."

"You're applying for jobs? In Billings?"

"Dad got an offer from the same cattle company leasing your land. If he takes it, and he thinks he will, we're going to be moving in a couple weeks."

Not thirty to sixty days.

The paper in Ace's hand dropped to the table. "You can't."

"Can't move?"

"I thought…you and I—"

"Nothing's changed."

"It has." They'd made love at Thunder Creek.

"Yes, all right. We're getting along. Which is what we wanted. We'll still get along when I live in Billings."

"I want to marry you."

"Do you love me?"

The question stunned him. "Of course," he stuttered.

Pain flared in her eyes.

He tried again, more convincingly. "I love you, Flynn. I do."

She nodded, compressed her lips together. "Didn't mean to drag it out of you."

"Dammit, I'm trying."

"You are. But loving someone, well, it shouldn't be something you have to struggle at. I know. I've been in love with you for a long time."

She had? She *had!*

"Then marry me and stay here."

"You're asking me to give up a lot."

"For us. For the baby."

"What are you going to give up? What sacrifice are you going to make?"

"Once the breeding business takes off, it'll be different. I'll have more time."

"In two or three years. You said so yourself."

He didn't respond, his previous joy deflating.

"As you can see, I have employment applications to complete," she said dismissively. "I'm sure you're tired after all the driving you did today."

Once again, Ace had handled the situation badly.

He got up. One look at her stoic features told him this was a discussion better left for another day.

"I'll see you tomorrow. For dinner."

"We don't have to go."

Yes, they did.

"I promised you. Uncle Joshua will be back from the rodeo and will cover for me. We won't have any interruptions."

"Fine."

She didn't need to tell him this was his last shot. Her tone said it all.

Chapter 15

A uniformed young man stepped out from behind a podium as Ace pulled up alongside the curb.

"Valet parking?" Flynn asked, mildly amused.

"We have a car tonight, I figured, why not."

They did indeed have a car. A Mustang. Convertible. It belonged to Harlan, one of the Harts' ranch hands. Ace had borrowed it. She didn't think she'd ever seen him drive anything but a truck or a tractor or that Polaris of his.

He looked good behind the wheel—and in

the charcoal-gray suit he'd worn. No cowboy hat and no boots, either. Another first.

She'd give credit where it was due. Ace had gone all out tonight to make the evening special for her. Car, clothes, swanky restaurant.

The one and only downside to the evening was her slinky maroon cocktail dress. It pinched uncomfortably in the middle.

Ace didn't appear to notice. He'd whistled appreciatively when he first saw her, his eyes eating her up like that key lime pie he favored.

She caught their reflection in the restaurant's glass entry doors and thought they made a striking couple, her poofy tummy aside.

Ace gave the hostess his name and after a short wait, during which they exchanged small talk with a couple celebrating a recent promotion, they were escorted to a booth by a window overlooking a lighted garden.

In the center of the table was a vase with a trio of red roses, around which had been tied a large silver bow. At first, Flynn assumed the arrangement was part of the restaurant's decor. Then she noticed the small envelope with her name on it.

"Are these from you?" she asked, already removing the card.

Ace didn't answer

"Three down, ninety-seven more to go," she read out loud, and smiled at the reference to the hundred-phone-call bet they'd made, flattered and touched. "Thank you."

"You're welcome."

"People are looking at us." She lifted the vase and brought the roses to her nose, inhaling their heady scent.

"They're looking at you, trying to figure out how a lug like me scored a date with such a beautiful lady."

She set the roses down. If anything, people were looking at Ace, an appealing combination of rugged handsomeness and polished sophistication. She wouldn't mind seeing him in a suit more often.

He might have better luck getting her to stay in Roundup and accept his proposal.

As yet, they hadn't discussed her seeking a job, nursing school, the lease for her father's land or her admission that she'd been in love with him for years. They would, eventually.

For the moment, Flynn enjoyed the roses and their easy conversation and the lovely view of the garden.

A waiter appeared. She and Ace placed their drink orders, a virgin margarita for her, and asked for more time to peruse the menu.

"Did you wind up watching the NASCAR races this afternoon?" she asked.

"For about an hour."

"Good." At least he'd gotten a little break from work.

"What about you?"

Flynn set her menu aside. Their reprieve from difficult conversation was apparently at an end. "I filled out employment applications, paper and online."

"How did that go?"

She could tell he strove to keep his voice neutral. "There really aren't a whole lot of opportunities out there. Not ones any better than what I have now, either paywise or interestingwise. I'd still rather go to school."

"Then do it."

"I have to work. Part-time, at least. Have to support myself while I take classes." And the baby. She didn't expect Ace to pay for everything.

She gave him credit for not mentioning she could come live with him and he'd support her.

"Interviewing for a job won't be easy," she

continued. "I know employers aren't supposed to discriminate, but the second they realize I'm pregnant, they'll probably choose another applicant."

Ace turned a page on his menu.

"No comment?" Flynn wondered if he was secretly glad of the obstacle she faced.

He gazed out the window. "It's staying light out a lot later these days."

Smart man.

The waiter returned with their drinks and took their orders.

"Are you still planning on being a nurse or just working?"

"I'm not sure."

The decision that was so simple six weeks ago had become complicated. Ace, the baby, Flynn's father retiring and leasing the ranch, all meddled with her thinking.

"You'd rather remain in the business admin side of the medical field?" Ace asked.

"Oh, no. I still want to do something more meaningful, more hands-on. Like you."

"Vaccinating calves and examining pregnant mares isn't what I'd call meaningful."

"Removing a malignant tumor from a child's beloved pony and giving him a few more years with his owner is. Curing my favorite horse of colic is. So is saving a family's pet dog."

"Lovey's life wasn't in danger."

"The Andersons didn't know that until you arrived." She sipped her drink. "That's the kind of rewarding work I want to do."

"Then go to veterinarian school."

She laughed. "I couldn't."

"Why not? You're smart. You love animals."

"I'm not cut out for surgery, no pun intended. I like assisting you. That part's fun. And interesting. And challenging."

"Then study to be a vet tech."

She started to protest, only to stop when chills ran up her arms. That wasn't such a bad idea. In fact, the more she thought about it, the more it appealed to her. She did love animals. She did like helping Ace. And working with people.

A vet tech. That was a degree she could probably obtain at community college. Far less difficult than getting into nursing school.

She could return to Billings Community College.

Roundup had a small community college, too, with online classes. She'd checked once.

Their dinner rolls arrived. Flynn was about

to question Ace about the requirements for becoming a vet tech when his cell phone rang.

She tensed. Oh, no! Not again.

He removed the phone from his jacket pocket and glanced at the caller ID. "It's Uncle Joshua." He hit the Disconnect button.

"You're not answering it?" She was amazed.

"He's filling in for me tonight." Ace set the phone on vibrate and laid it beside his plate. "Whatever problem he has, he can resolve it without me."

Wow. This was a pleasant change of pace.

"How long does it usually take to become a vet tech?"

"Depends on the school." Ace had barely started to explain when his phone went off again. He studied the display a moment longer than before, then disconnected.

"Uncle Joshua again?"

"Yes." This time, Ace slipped the phone in his shirt pocket, his facial muscles taut.

"If you want to call him, go ahead."

"I promised, no interruptions tonight." He grabbed a dinner roll and buttered it, his movements stilted.

His phone vibrated again, humming like an angry hornet.

"I'm going to turn this off." He whipped

the phone out of his pocket, only to pause. "It's Dinah."

The few bites Flynn had taken of her roll turned to lead in her stomach. Something was wrong. "You'd better get it."

Ace clearly felt the same way, for he answered his phone with a brusque, "Hey, sis." As he listened, his face drained of color. "I'll be right there."

"What's the matter?" Flynn asked when he started to rise.

"It's Mom. She's been taken to the hospital. They think she's had a heart attack."

Flynn walked the empty barn. All her father's horses were gone. The bulls, too. A rodeo stock contractor from Idaho had purchased the remaining few head, picking them up this morning.

This morning had also been when her father had received a lease agreement from the Missoula Cattle Company via email and made an appointment with a local attorney to review it.

The wheels were in motion. In a few weeks, her father would be moving to Billings. He couldn't wait. She, on the other hand, was still undecided about what to do.

One minute, remaining in Roundup with Ace, attending Roundup Community College, felt right. The next minute, she was convinced staying would simply delay the inevitable.

Why hadn't he called?

She'd taken a cab home from the hospital about two o'clock last night. By then, Sarah was in stable condition and resting comfortably, her family by her bedside—Ace, Dinah, Joshua, Beau, Duke and Colt, who'd arrived at the hospital about one o'clock. Tuf had yet to be located, though the family continued trying.

She hoped for Sarah's sake they reached him soon. Constantly worrying about his whereabouts had no doubt contributed to her heart attack.

Maybe Flynn shouldn't have left the hospital. Ace had insisted she go home, telling her there was no point in hanging around. His mother was, according to the doctor, out of danger and ready to be moved to a regular room. One of them should get some sleep.

Flynn left only after Ace agreed to call her bright and early. She'd slept very little, rising soon after dawn, her eyes gritty, her worry for all the Harts a throbbing ache in her chest.

A glance at her phone confirmed that she hadn't missed a call from Ace in the fifteen minutes since she last checked her phone.

Where was he?

Maybe Sarah was better, and he'd gone home to get some sleep.

What if she was worse?

I won't leave Roundup, Flynn thought. Ace might need her. At least until Sarah was well. The cattle company didn't want the house. Flynn could research vet tech degrees, finish packing, decide her future course once and for all.

Give Ace more time to convince her to marry him.

More time to fall in love with her. *Really* fall in love, not just say the words because she'd put him on the spot.

What about the hundred phone calls? The roses? The afternoon at Thunder Creek making love?

If those weren't an indication he had strong feelings for her, what was?

Three little words. Until he spoke them straight from the heart, Flynn wouldn't be entirely sure if what he felt for her was enough to last a lifetime. Enough to guarantee he wouldn't abandon her like her ex-husband and mother had done.

Like Ace had done ten years ago.

The echo of footsteps had her whirling toward the barn entrance, her pulse thrumming.

"Ace!"

He stood in the shadows, an inky silhouette against a dim backdrop. Still, she instantly recognized him.

She ran toward him, threw her arms around his neck.

"How's your mom?"

"Better. They're going to keep her a day or two for observation. Run some more tests."

He squeezed her tight as if this was what he'd been waiting for all day, all night. Flynn forgot her worry, forgot how tired she was and hugged him back.

"That's not too bad for a heart attack," she said into his rumpled dress shirt.

"She didn't have one. Not technically." They drew apart and walked hand in hand out of the barn into the sunlight. "She has angina."

"I…don't know what that is."

"It's a sign of trouble. Sort of like a pre-heart attack. Definitely her body giving her a warning. She may require a stent. We'll know more later today."

"How's she handling the news?"

"All right. The cardiac surgeon is very optimistic that with the right treatment and adequate rest she'll be fine."

"Will she be on medication?"

"Yeah. The doctor said it might take a few weeks to find the right combination. He warned her, warned *all* of us, that unless she makes some serious lifestyle changes, she could have another episode."

"Changes like diet?"

"Lots of food restrictions, apparently. Mom will not be happy. Exercise, too. The right kind. And here's the hardest part. Reduce her stress levels."

"Oh, Ace." Flynn hugged him again. "She's going to be all right. That's the important part."

"She has to be careful the rest of her life or else the angina can develop into a serious heart condition."

"Your mother's very conscientious. Plus, she has her family to watch out for her."

Ace let go of Flynn's hand, his features clouding.

She knew instantly something else was wrong. "What is it?"

"The doctor was adamant. Mom has to drastically minimize her stress."

"Maybe if you can find Tuf, get him to come home, she won't worry as much."

"That's definitely the first item on my list, but not the only one."

It was coming. Another breakup. He had the same distant look in his eyes, the same tightness in his voice, the same stiff posture from ten years ago.

No! her mind screamed, so loud it surprised her when her voice came out calm and even. "You have to take over for her."

"I don't have a choice. I'm the only one who can do it."

Just like when his father died. Ace, the ever loyal son. Except when it came to Flynn.

"But you're not the only one," she said.

"Who else is there? Tuf is gone. Dinah has her job as sheriff, which is pretty much 24/7. Colt is undependable. At least he has been up till now."

"Talk to him. He may step up if you ask him."

"He didn't when Dad died."

"What about your practice?"

"I'll have to refer some of my customers to another vet."

"But you've worked so hard."

"My family's entire future is at stake. If we don't make a success of the contracting and breeding business, don't pay down the loan, I won't have a practice to worry about."

"What about us?" Flynn asked in that same calm, steady voice.

"Please be patient with me. I'll be there as much as I can for you and the baby, but I probably won't have time to go out like we've been doing. Not for a while."

"I don't care about going out. That was never important to me. I like being with you. Working with you. Hanging out with you."

"Let me see how it goes." He rubbed his temples and exhaled wearily. "We have to determine the extent of Mom's care before I make any decisions. And her workload. Where we stand with our current stock contracts, the financials, the alfalfa crop."

It seemed to Flynn the choice of whether to stay or go had been made for her.

She glanced away to hide her hurt and disappointment. "Call me if you need anything. I'll be packing over the next few days."

"You're moving?" He looked stunned, as if they hadn't had this same conversation a dozen times already.

"Don't you think it's for the best?" She cleared her throat. It didn't dislodge the burning lump stuck there. "I don't want to add to your problems."

"You're not a problem."

"We can talk when you're not so tired."

"I don't want you to move."

"You just said you didn't think you'd have time for me. Which I completely understand."

"Give me a couple weeks."

"What difference would it make? Your responsibilities don't come with an expiration date."

"I have a responsibility to you and the baby, too."

"The difference is we can get along without you. The same isn't true for your mother."

"I'm going to be an involved father."

"When are you going to fit me and the baby in your schedule? A week from Tuesday?"

"I can't support a baby, can't do right by him or her, if the business fails."

"He or she will need more from you than

a weekly child support check." Flynn needed more, too.

"Why does it have to be all or nothing with you? Why do I have to choose between my work and my family and you?"

"Because love and marriage and raising a child is a full-time commitment. I won't settle for less."

"I'm not Paul."

"No, you're not. He didn't have a family depending on him like you. On the other hand, he didn't have a baby on the way, either."

"That's not fair."

"Our child deserves the best from *both* his parents. Problem is you're only capable of giving a limited amount."

"For now," he insisted.

"Fine. You can give what you're able to just as easily in Billings as here. Easier, in fact. Sleep on it. You'll see the rationale when you're not so exhausted."

She started to walk away.

He didn't follow. "You're being selfish."

"Me!" That stopped her in her tracks.

"You can't expect a man not to have other responsibilities besides you."

"I have other responsibilities, too. Yet,

I don't let them consume me to the exclusion of everything else. The entire fate of the Harts doesn't rest entirely on your shoulders, Ace. It never has, not even when your dad died. You've just convinced yourself it does."

"Who would run things if I didn't?"

"You've never given anyone else a chance." Her voice rose. "I don't know why I missed seeing it before, but you know what? You use your work and your family as an excuse not to fall in love. Not to commit."

"That's ridiculous."

"Is it? Just think. Whenever you're in danger of getting close to me, I'm not talking about marriage but emotionally close, you suddenly have more responsibilities. Another iron in the fire. Sorry, Flynn, can't be with you because I'm too busy."

She was allowing her anger to get the best of her. Reining it in, however, wasn't possible.

"There can't be any future for us," she said. "Not until you stop being afraid."

"Maybe your expectations are unrealistic."

Finally! Something he said made sense.

"Maybe they are. Or maybe yours are. We'll probably never find out. I'll call you before my doctor's appointment next week. In case you want to go with me."

This time when she walked away, he didn't call her back.

Chapter 16

Ace absently patted Midnight's neck, then caught himself as Fancy Gal nudged his arm, demanding her share of attention.

The stallion was standing next to him, allowing Ace to touch him! And without Ace having to coax him with a carrot.

Another day, a different time, Ace would have broken into an ear-to-ear grin and congratulated himself on his success. All his efforts, his endless hours, had finally paid off.

Except he wasn't much in the mood for grinning and hadn't been since Flynn left him to stew alone in her father's barn.

They'd spoken in the eight days following

their argument. On the phone, not in person. About her next doctor's appointment. About how she was feeling. About his mother's prognosis and adjustment now that she was home from the hospital. About Flynn's decision to obtain her vet tech degree and how that was proceeding—much more swiftly than nursing school.

What they didn't talk about was their situation. If Ace tried to bring up anything remotely personal, she promptly ended their conversation. As a result, he'd stuck strictly to safe topics and kept his frustrations to himself.

He wasn't a content man. He was, in fact, miserable and fairly certain he'd made the worst mistake anyone could by not going after her.

All he'd wanted was to marry Flynn and provide for her and their child. Instead, he'd hurt her. Alienated her. Convinced her to doubt his feelings for her rather than to rely on them.

Ace shut the lid on his medical case, untied Fancy Gal's lead rope and removed her halter. He'd spent the last two hours making the rounds of the ranch, examining the first two rotations of mares that had been pastured with Midnight. Seven of them, including Fancy Gal, were pregnant.

Yet more reason to celebrate. Not exactly the auspicious start to their breeding business Ace and his mother had originally planned for, but, assuming more mares were bred, they'd be guaranteed a sizable crop of foals next spring.

Ace would feel better if their mare motel was filled to capacity with customers' horses and Midnight relied on to hand breed with them.

No, not even that would make him feel better.

Why hadn't he told Flynn he loved her when he had the chance? In such a way she would have believed him.

Ace gave Midnight and Fancy Gal a final pat on their rumps, rewarding them for standing quietly during his examination of Fancy Gal.

"Congratulations you two, you're going to be parents. Well, buddy, in your case, a parent many times over." Midnight nosed Ace's empty shirt pocket. "Consider yourself lucky your girl here's not the jealous type."

When the stallion's search failed to produce a treat, he snorted angrily.

"Sorry, fresh out of carrots." Ace scratched the horse's nose, wishing he could marvel at this advancement. "Eventually I'm going to have to separate you two. When she's closer to foaling."

Midnight abruptly meandered off.

"Hey," Ace called after him. "Don't be mad. I understand how you feel. I'm in the same boat. My girl's having a baby, and I can't be with her."

Whose fault was that?

"Talking to horses now?"

Ace pivoted at the sound of his brother's voice. That explained Midnight's sudden departure. The horse still didn't like anyone except Gracie and, apparently, Ace.

"What are you doing here?" A thought galvanized him. "Is Mom okay?"

"She's fine," Colt said agreeably. "Supervising the woman you hired to help with the laundry and housework. Complaining up a storm that you're a dictator who won't even allow her on the computer."

"Let her complain." Ace grabbed his medical case and met up with Colt on the other side of the gate. "I'll take that as a sign she's feeling better."

They headed toward Ace's truck, which

he'd parked nearby. Now that he was finished checking the mares, he had several appointments, appointments he should have gotten to yesterday but had run out of daylight.

"She's worried about you," Colt said.

"Don't know why. I'm not the one who nearly had a heart attack."

"You might be, at the rate you're going."

Rather than answer, Ace loaded his medical case in the side compartment on his truck.

"Come on, you're a wreck. Have you looked in the mirror lately?"

Ace had. That morning. A stranger stared back at him—one with a four-day growth of beard, dark circles beneath his eyes and a rather unflattering grayish complexion.

"I don't have time for this," he grumbled.

Before he could jump into his truck, Colt grabbed his arm. "Hey, wait a minute."

"I'm running late."

"Talk to me."

"Aren't you leaving for Utah today?"

"I canceled."

"What about qualifying for the NFR? I thought you were behind in steer wrestling and bull riding."

"It won't hurt me to take some time off."

Ace wished his brother had said that weeks ago. Years ago.

"I thought maybe we could go out for a beer tonight."

"A beer?" Ace couldn't remember going out for a beer with his brother for…ages.

They weren't close. Not like they should be. Not like when they were younger.

All of them, including their mother, were casualties of John Hart's life and his death. The man had left a legacy, just not the one he'd intended.

"I'm not good company," Ace said, sliding in behind the steering wheel.

"I know you've been down since Flynn dumped you."

The bluntness of Colt's remark stung.

"And you wonder why I don't want to go out with you."

"I can help you."

"With what?"

"Whatever you need. You're working too hard."

"Mom put you up to this?"

"She and I might have talked."

"That's what I figured."

"She's right. You need a break before you kill yourself."

"I like working. It keeps me out of trouble."

"Keeps you from hurting, too. It was the same when Dad died. The busier you are, the less you have to think. Feel."

"I don't need you to psychoanalyze me, too."

"Too? Who else has been doing it?"

"No one." Flynn's comments from the other day were still eating at Ace, and he'd be damned if he was going to discuss them. Especially with Colt.

"Was it by chance—"

"You'll shut up if you know what's good for you."

"Why won't you let me help you?" his brother demanded.

"The truth? I've counted on you before, and you've let me down. Let the family down. It's just simpler if I, if I—" Ace stopped in mid-sentence, momentarily struck dumb.

"What? Simpler if you do it yourself? Is that what you were going to say?"

It had been.

Up until this second, Ace hadn't noticed the similarities between his relationship with Flynn and his relationship with his brother. Now, it stared him in the face. His beard-stubbled, gray face.

He'd disappointed Flynn, and she didn't trust him. Just like he didn't trust Colt.

Ace sure didn't like what he was learning about himself lately.

Maybe if he gave his brother another chance, Flynn would do the same for him. Did karma work like that?

It was worth a try, he supposed. And he did need help. Even if Colt relieved him of only one or two tasks, it would lighten his load. Enable Ace to hit the sack earlier—so he'd have even more time to stare at the ceiling instead of sleeping.

He grabbed a pad of paper and pen off the seat beside him. Scratching out several notes, he ripped the sheet of paper from the pad and handed it to Colt.

"Take care of these for me."

Colt scanned the list, his brow crinkling. "Research prices on breeding mounts? Wait. Is this what I think it is?"

"The season will be over soon. We have to do something with Midnight the rest of the year. I'm thinking artificial insemination. In order to do that, we're going to have to train him to use a mount and to collect the—"

"I get it. You don't have to draw me a picture."

"Mom was going to call the grain distributers this week and get prices. You can do it for her."

Colt gave Ace a smart salute. "See you when you get home, boss."

Ace started to tell his brother not to flake. Instead, he clamped his mouth shut, hearing their father's voice inside his head saying those exact words. *Shouting* those exact words. At him.

He wouldn't treat Colt the same way he'd been treated.

Whatever it took, he'd be a better parent to his son or daughter than John Hart ever was. He wouldn't put his family in financial jeopardy and expect them to fend for themselves. He wouldn't drink in solitude rather than spend time with his wife and baby. He'd be there always. Responsible. Dependable. Loyal.

Weren't those the same qualities that had driven Flynn away?

Ace left the ranch and headed for his first appointment at the local riding stables. Angie's animal rescue shelter was his last scheduled stop for the day. He didn't leave there until well after 6:00 p.m. On the way home, an idea occurred to him and quickly took shape.

Ignoring his debilitating exhaustion, he went straight to the family room upon returning home, looking for his mother. She was resting on the couch, the TV blaring, a bored expression on her face. It beat the heck out of the pale, taut expression she'd worn the days following her angina episode, made worse by their inability to locate Tuf.

When his youngest brother finally did come home, he'd have a lot of explaining to do—after which, Ace was going to kick Tuf's ass all the way to the center of town.

"What have you been up to while I was gone?" he asked, striding into the room.

"Aidan! You're home." His mother pushed to a sitting position, picked up the remote control and silenced the TV. "I've been up to nothing at all, thanks to you, Mr. Warden." Her smile turned to a mock frown. "You're going to have to grant me parole soon."

"That's just what I had in mind."

She brightened. "At last!"

"I was at the animal shelter this afternoon. They're really understaffed. I was thinking you could volunteer there a couple mornings a week or something."

"Volunteer?"

"Sure." He sat on the couch next to her. "It would get you out of the house. Give you a chance to be physically active without over-extending yourself. And I think working with the puppies and kittens will be good for you. Mentally and emotionally."

"I can't possibly. Once I get back to work—"

"When you get back, it'll be on a part-time basis."

"Only temporarily."

"We'll see."

"Aidan." She said his name in that way mothers tended to do.

"Come on. Angie can use the help."

"It's not right. You're doing the job of two people." She pointed at the TV. "And I'm watching game shows."

"Colt is helping me."

"He is?"

"I'm waiting to see how that goes."

"I bet he'll surprise you."

"I hope he does."

His mother pursed her mouth thoughtfully. "What if I get attached to the animals?"

"Adopt one."

"I haven't wanted another dog since old Buster passed away last year."

"People who own pets live longer. It's a proven fact."

"So do people who are happy."

He intentionally took her remark the wrong way. "All the more reason to get a dog."

"Okay, okay. You've convinced me. When do I start?"

"As soon as the doctor clears you."

"How are you doing?" She studied him critically. "You look terrible. Are you sleeping? Eating enough?"

"Yes and yes." Just not much, which he was sure his mother had already figured out. "I'm going to hit the shower, then the office. Pay some bills. Place some orders online."

"What about dinner?"

He rubbed the back of his neck where the muscles ached. "I'll grab a sandwich after I clean up. Take it with me to the office."

"It's not my place to tell you how to run your life, but I'm going to anyway."

"Mom, not now."

"You have to make some changes."

"I am. I gave Colt a list."

"That's fine. It's also not enough. You have to delegate," she continued. "You can't go on, carrying the entire burden of this family.

Doing my job and yours. You have a life of your own, a baby on the way."

"Everyone else has their own life, too."

"They can do more. I've asked them already," she said proudly, "since I'm sure you won't."

"Right, Colt."

"And Joshua and Dinah. Beau and Duke, too."

"Mom—"

"They want to help. That's what family does for each other."

"I can handle things."

"Stop, Aidan. This isn't a criticism. Far from it. You do an amazing job. I couldn't possibly have run this ranch all these years without you. But Flynn needs you. Your child needs you. More than we do."

"What about your angina?"

"I'm going to be fine. All I need is a little rest." She squeezed his hand, brought it to her cheek. "We're going to get through this, like we always have. Together."

The doorbell rang, and Ace rose.

"It's all right." She pulled on his wrist. "Lisa Marie will answer the door. Probably the UPS man. He's always late."

Lisa Marie? Oh, yeah. The woman he'd hired to help with the housework.

He really was tired.

"Shower and eat," his mother told him. "A real meal, not a sandwich. Then call Flynn."

"She won't talk to me. Not about what's important."

"Then maybe you should go there. Refuse to leave until she listens. This constant working, it isn't good for you. Take it from me. Too much responsibility is what drove your father to drink. To push you kids too hard. Turn his back on the ranch. Turn his back on me."

Was that true?

His father had definitely changed the last few years of his life.

"I don't want you to end up like him," his mother said softly. "Flynn is a wonderful girl, and you're going to have a beautiful baby. My first grandchild." Her eyes misted. "It would devastate me if I couldn't see the baby because you and Flynn weren't on speaking terms."

"I screwed up with her." Ace scrubbed his face, the beard feeling strange scratching his palms. "Really screwed up."

"Then apologize."

"I have."

"Apologize again. However many times as it takes."

"I love her, you know. I think I always have."

"I do know. I could see it."

"I was afraid to tell her how I felt. I always thought there was no way this incredible woman could possibly return my feelings."

"She does. I could see that, too."

He took off his hat, wiped his eyes and nose with his shirt sleeve. "There isn't anything I wouldn't do for her."

"Tell her." His mother's glance cut briefly to the entryway. "It's not too late."

"She's leaving next week."

"But she's here now."

"And refusing to see me."

"No." His mother tilted her head toward the entryway. "I mean, she's here now. Right here."

Ace turned and stared at Flynn, the shock of seeing her sending a jolt tearing through him.

She stood in the entryway, her father beside her. He held a card and a large, leafy floral arrangement.

How much of what Ace had said to his mother had she heard?

Judging by the startled look in her eyes, most of it.

"Well, don't sit there like a bump on a log," his mother whispered. "Here's your chance."

Who was he to disobey his mother?

Flynn's heart soared. She pressed a hand to her chest in a feeble attempt to contain it.

Ace loved her! He wasn't just saying what he thought she wanted to hear or what might convince her to marry him. And he'd loved her for a long time.

Why hadn't he told her before? What a difference it would have made in their lives.

"You going to just stand here?" her father asked. "Or are you going to put him out of his misery?"

"I… I…"

Ace approached her. Her heart might be soaring but, for the first time, his was right there on his sleeve for all to see.

"Flynn. You're here."

"To visit your mother."

She'd imagined running into him, imagined what she'd say. But that had been before she overheard him tell his mother he loved her.

They stood facing each other, Flynn acutely aware of their parents' curious stares.

Her father must have grown tired of waiting, for he stepped around her. "Sarah, it's good to see you." He held out the plant and card. "How are you doing?"

"I'm well." She stood and accepted the gift. "Thank you, Earl."

"Doesn't appear as if these two are going to settle their differences on their own. Not without a little help from us."

She smiled. "What were you thinking?"

"Have you had your dinner yet?"

"I was waiting for Aidan."

"What do you say we grab a bite somewhere? My treat. If we take my truck, Flynn can't leave. That ought to force 'em to talk to each other."

"I admire a man with a plan."

"No, don't! There's something I want to say first." Flynn swallowed, gathered her courage, which she'd never needed more. "I've been selfish. I didn't realize until now that this baby isn't mine alone or even mine and Ace's alone." She turned to him, then to his mother. "If I move, I won't just be taking him away from his father, but from his grandmother and uncles and aunt, too."

"He'll also have family in Billings," Sarah said gently. "Your sister and, before long, your father, too."

"That's exactly my point. Dad will have my sister and her sons." Flynn touched Sarah's arm fondly. "If I move, you won't have any grandchildren nearby."

"Oh, Flynn." Sarah's hand fluttered to her throat.

"I don't understand." Ace's rough and gravelly voice didn't sound at all like him. "Are you staying in Roundup?"

"Yes, I am."

She took his hands in hers, marveled again at how they could be both strong and gentle. Grip the rigging on a wildly bucking bronc or tenderly bandage a dog's injured foot. Twist a wrench to loosen a frozen lug nut or explore her body with shiver-inducing caresses.

Soon, his hands would hold their baby.

"If you do stay," Ace said, "it has to be for me. Us. Not for my mother or any guilt you might have."

"I could live with guilt." Flynn sought his gaze and held it steady. "What I can't do is live without you."

"I love you, Flynn."

This time she not only heard the words, she felt them deep inside her, echoing until they matched the rhythm of her heartbeat.

"I love you, too."

Suddenly he was holding her, and they sealed their declarations with a kiss that would have lasted longer if not for Flynn's father clearing his throat. Loudly.

"If you meant what you said earlier about doing anything for me..."

"I did. I'll work less, cut back on my vet practice—"

"The working less part is okay." She touched his cheek with its dark, scratchy stubble. Later she'd tell him how sexy he looked. "But don't cut back on your vet practice. I have a better idea. Let me help you. I'll run the office and assist you on calls. In between, I'll go to school."

He smiled broadly. "Deal."

"You haven't heard my list of demands yet."

His brows rose. "Demands?"

"For starters, you're going to have to do something about that ancient piece of junk you call a computer. And your filing system." She rolled her eyes.

"Is that all? Because I have my own demands."

Did he now?

"What are they?"

"Date night once a week, including after the baby's born. And Sundays are family day. No work unless there's an extreme emergency, and I mean extreme. At least one Sunday every month we visit your family in Billings."

"I think we can manage that." She blinked the tears from her eyes.

Sarah, too.

"There's one more piece of business we have to get out of the way," Ace announced.

"Business?"

He turned to her father. "Earl, I intend to marry your daughter. I'd like your blessing."

Sarah gasped with delight and clapped her hands together.

"Well." Flynn's father rubbed his chin as if considering his answer. "That's really up to my daughter. I'm not sure she'll have you after what you've put her through over the years."

Sarah punched him lightly in the arm. "Earl."

"Well, he's not the easiest man to get along with."

"And you are?"

He shrugged.

"Answer him," Sarah insisted.

"You going to do right by her?" he asked Ace. "Take care of her? Because if you don't, I'll—"

"Dad!" Flynn laughed. "Enough."

She sobered when Ace drew her into his arms.

"I'll take care of her. Count on it." He spoke as if they were the only two people in the room. In the world. "You're everything to me, Flynn. Every time I see you, every time I kiss you, it's like falling in love all over again."

Her knees wobbled. If he'd proposed to her like that before, she'd have said yes.

"Say you'll marry me." He bent and brushed his lips across hers in the lightest, tenderest of kisses. "I'll ask you a hundred times, a thousand times, if that's what it takes."

"Yes. Yes, yes, *yes!*"

"Did you hear?" Sarah grabbed Flynn's father by the arm. "She accepted!"

"I heard, I heard." He pretended to scowl. The glimmer in his eyes gave him away.

Flynn paid them little attention. She was

too preoccupied kissing her fiancé and letting him sweep her off her feet—literally.

Ace had scooped her into his arms and was twirling her in circles. The room was spinning when he finally put her down. Then he kissed her again, deeply and fully, and she realized it was Ace and their love, not the twirling, that made her dizzy.

"I can't wait to spend the rest of our lives together," she whispered in his ear.

"And here I thought you accepted my proposal in order to guarantee yourself a job when you finish school."

"What!" She squirmed.

He didn't release her, pinning her to him until she stopped protesting.

"Come on, Sarah," Flynn's father said. "Let's get out of here and have that dinner. I'm starving."

"We'll come with you," Ace said.

"Stay," Sarah said. "You have plans to make."

"I want to celebrate," Ace insisted. "And I can't think of a better place than the Number 1 Diner. Call the rest of the family. Tell them to meet us there. We'll make an announcement."

The place where it had all started just three short months ago.

That seemed entirely appropriate, Flynn thought as she and Ace walked arm in arm out the door and into their future.

Epilogue

"Mom, don't overdo IT," Ace warned. "Slow down already."

"Stop fussing." His mother waved him away. "It's your wedding day. You should be thinking about your bride. Not me."

"My wife," he corrected, liking the sound of it. "And I am thinking about her."

His glance strayed to Flynn, who was huddled with Nora and Dinah. Her sister and brand-new sister-in-law were fawning over the diamond ring Ace had recently purchased and Flynn's dress, which had belonged to Ace's mother and was hastily altered to fit Flynn.

"She's beautiful," his mother said, linking her arm through his. "I'm glad you both finally came to your senses."

"She is beautiful." With Flynn for a mother, their baby—Ace was still hoping for a girl—couldn't be anything but gorgeous.

"Are you ready to cut the cake?"

"Almost." Ace wanted to spend just a few more minutes enjoying the reception from where he stood.

His mother and sister had done an amazing job, pulling the wedding together in just ten days. Though dark clouds gathered overhead, the weather had thankfully cooperated, and the ceremony went off without a hitch.

Ace and Flynn had chosen not to wait and opted for a simple civil ceremony in the Harts' spacious front yard. Red checkered cloths covered the tables, enough to accommodate the hundred and fifty guests in attendance. Paper flowers taped to the backs of chairs fluttered in the breeze. Children clambered on and over the bales of straw that had been arranged in a semicircle to create a makeshift altar.

Most of the guests were complaining of overeating. Blame the barbecue beef and chicken and the best coleslaw anyone had ever tasted. Flynn's father's secret recipe.

The day was almost perfect, and would be if not for the two empty chairs at the wedding party table.

Both Ace's brothers were absent. They still hadn't been able to locate Tuf. Neither had he called them. And Colt… Ace didn't know what to think.

His brother had promised to be at the wedding, was supposed to serve as Ace's best man. Only Colt hadn't come home last night, wasn't answering his cell phone and wasn't returning the countless messages Ace had left. Finally, an hour before the ceremony, Ace had asked his cousin Duke to stand in for him.

Colt had been stepping up the past week, lending Ace a hand with the work around the ranch. But now this. He'd evidently returned to his old ways.

Ace was angry and disappointed and frustrated. Mostly, he was hurt and sad. Today was his wedding day, the only one he intended to have, and his brothers had missed it.

"Hey, you two." Flynn strolled over to join Ace and his mother.

He couldn't immediately speak, his breath

having left his lungs in a soft rush. She had that effect on him, and he hoped it lasted forever.

Thoughts of his brothers fled. This was their day, his and Flynn's. They would enjoy every moment of it and let nothing interfere.

"Flynn," his mother said, "I was just asking Ace. Are you ready to cut the cake?"

"Thank you, Sarah, for everything you've done." Flynn hugged her. "I hope you'll let me return the favor."

"You already have. You're giving me my first grandchild."

"Would you like to come with Ace and I to the doctor's office next month? We're having another ultrasound."

His mother's face positively glowed, and she grasped Flynn to her. "I would like that very much."

Flynn's father came over. He placed an affectionate hand on Sarah's shoulder. "Did I miss something?"

"I'm just being a sentimental fool."

"I think you're rather charming."

Ace almost did a double take. Was Earl flirting with his mother? A quick check with Flynn assured him she'd noticed something, too.

Well, his mother could do worse, if she

was indeed interested in Earl. And Earl couldn't do any better than Ace's mother.

"When are you leaving?" Earl asked.

"Around six."

Ace and Flynn were spending four days at a luxury inn in Billings. He'd wanted to take her on a longer, more exciting honeymoon, but that would have to wait a while. Flynn had yet to finalize her schedule for school, which would start this fall, and Ace still had to move.

They were going to live in Earl's house. He'd generously offered to rent it to them at a reasonable rate. Eventually, when the loan Ace and his mother had taken out was paid off and Earl's land lease with the cattle company was at an end, Ace intended to buy the entire ranch from his father-in-law.

In the months to come he'd move up his vet practice to Earl's barn. For now, Ace was leaving it here, close to Midnight, the mares and the bucking stock.

Suddenly, thunder rumbled ominously overhead.

"Uh-oh." His mother peered at the sky with its ever darkening clouds. "We'd better hurry with the cake."

More photographs were snapped as Ace

and Flynn stuffed cake into each other's mouths. The guests had barely finished eating when the skies opened up and let loose with a magnificent downpour.

People scrambled and scurried in a dozen different directions, carrying leftover food inside, collecting trash before it blew away and removing tablecloths and serving dishes.

Ace grabbed Flynn's hand and started running.

"Where are we going?" she gasped.

"To the barn."

"What about our guests? The gifts."

"Later."

Clothes soaked and their breath coming in bursts, they ducked into the barn and stood just inside the entrance, watching the rain come down and listening to it strike the roof with a mighty force.

Like the night Ace had kissed her in his truck outside the diner.

Flynn must have been remembering as well, for she grabbed the lapels of his Western-cut suit jacket and pulled him toward her. "Did I tell you how handsome you look today?"

"Did I tell you how much I love you?"

"Yes." She snuggled against him. "But you can say it again. I won't complain."

"I am without a doubt the luckiest guy in the world."

Wrapping her and their unborn child in his embrace, he kissed her. Their second one as husband and wife.

"Two down." He nuzzled her ear. "And a million or more to go."

* * * * *

Get 4 FREE REWARDS!

We'll send you 2 FREE Books plus 2 FREE Mystery Gifts.

FREE
Value Over
$20

Both the **Romance** and **Suspense** collections feature compelling novels written by many of today's bestselling authors.

YES! Please send me 2 FREE novels from the Essential Romance or Essential Suspense Collection and my 2 FREE gifts (gifts are worth about $10 retail). After receiving them, if I don't wish to receive any more books, I can return the shipping statement marked "cancel." If I don't cancel, I will receive 4 brand-new novels every month and be billed just $7.24 each in the U.S. or $7.49 each in Canada. That's a savings of up to 38% off the cover price. It's quite a bargain! Shipping and handling is just 50¢ per book in the U.S. and $1.25 per book in Canada.* I understand that accepting the 2 free books and gifts places me under no obligation to buy anything. I can always return a shipment and cancel at any time by calling the number below. The free books and gifts are mine to keep no matter what I decide.

Choose one: ☐ **Essential Romance**　　☐ **Essential Suspense**
　　　　　　　　(194/394 MDN GQ6M)　　　(191/391 MDN GQ6M)

Name (please print)

Address　　　　　　　　　　　　　　　　　　　　　　　　　Apt. #

City　　　　　　　　　　State/Province　　　　　　　　Zip/Postal Code

Email: Please check this box ☐ if you would like to receive newsletters and promotional emails from Harlequin Enterprises ULC and its affiliates. You can unsubscribe anytime.

Mail to the **Harlequin Reader Service:**
IN U.S.A.: P.O. Box 1341, Buffalo, NY 14240-8531
IN CANADA: P.O. Box 603, Fort Erie, Ontario L2A 5X3

Want to try 2 free books from another series! Call 1-800-873-8635 or visit www.ReaderService.com.

*Terms and prices subject to change without notice. Prices do not include sales taxes, which will be charged (if applicable) based on your state or country of residence. Canadian residents will be charged applicable taxes. Offer not valid in Quebec. This offer is limited to one order per household. Books received may not be as shown. Not valid for current subscribers to the Essential Romance or Essential Suspense Collection. All orders subject to approval. Credit or debit balances in a customer's account(s) may be offset by any other outstanding balance owed by or to the customer. Please allow 4 to 6 weeks for delivery. Offer available while quantities last.

Your Privacy—Your information is being collected by Harlequin Enterprises ULC, operating as Harlequin Reader Service. For a complete summary of the information we collect, how we use this information and to whom it is disclosed, please visit our privacy notice located at corporate.harlequin.com/privacy-notice. From time to time we may also exchange your personal information with reputable third parties. If you wish to opt out of this sharing of your personal information, please visit readerservice.com/consumerschoice or call 1-800-873-8635. **Notice to California Residents**—Under California law, you have specific rights to control and access your data. For more information on these rights and how to exercise them, visit corporate.harlequin.com/california-privacy.

STRS22R2

Get 4 FREE REWARDS!

We'll send you 2 FREE Books plus 2 FREE Mystery Gifts.

FREE Value Over **$20**

Both the **Harlequin Intrigue®** and **Harlequin® Romantic Suspense** series feature compelling novels filled with heart-racing action-packed romance that will keep you on the edge of your seat.

HARLEQUIN
PLUS

Announcing a **BRAND-NEW** multimedia subscription service for romance fans like you!

Read, Watch and Play.

Experience the easiest way to get the romance content you crave.

Start your **FREE 7 DAY TRIAL** at www.harlequinplus.com/freetrial.